In the dense black smoke from the guns, the two ships came together. The grapnels were thrown, the two hulls lashed.

"Boarders!" Casca ordered and, cutlass in hand, leaped for the other deck, Katie beside him, her own cutlass at the ready.

"There's something wrong, Scarface," she muttered. "Why didn't he fire on us?"

There wasn't time for him to answer. He jumped aboard the ship, Katie Parnell matching him step for step, and for the first time in his life Casca Rufio Longinus felt the odd pleasure of going into battle with a woman he trusted. . . .

The Casca series
by Barry Sadler

CASCA:

THE PIRATE

BARRY SADLER #15

J

JOVE BOOKS, NEW YORK

CASCA #15: THE PIRATE

A Jove Book / published by arrangement with
the author

PRINTING HISTORY
Charter edition / December 1985
Jove edition / September 1987

ISBN: 0-515-09599-0

Jove Books are published by The Berkley Publishing Group,
200 Madison Avenue, New York, New York 10016.
The name "JOVE" and the "J" logo
are trademarks belonging to Jove Publications, Inc.

PRINTED IN THE UNITED STATES OF AMERICA

10   9   8   7   6   5   4

THE PIRATE

CHAPTER ONE

The long gray fingers of the tropical dawn fondled the island of Jamaica, and caught in their thin embrace was the shifting figure of the man who had penetrated the defenses of McAdams' compound. The man—the intruder—had but little time to gain access to McAdams' bedroom. Dawn here was quick—like a reluctant lover anxious to get it over with—and the man had to make haste. And this one did; he knew his business. He was an old pro. And in this, the year of our Lord 1718, when most of the world—as usual—had their heads in their asses, knowing one's business was a big advantage.

The intruder needed an advantage. In fact he needed all the help he could get. McAdams' compound was high up in the Blue Mountains, and every damn inch of it was under the eyes of guards. And there were the dogs.

The intruder knew about the failings of human guards, and he knew about dogs. Men tended to relax when the dawn's groping fingers touched them—unless they were very well trained, which he doubted these were. And as for the dogs, he had picked the leeward side of the coming sea breeze. They would not pick up his scent.

However, one dog did catch a brief trace of something, came to attention and looked to the half-darkness. But the scent was confusing, and the dog shared the guards' indolence; he lay back down.

Two of the sentries saw a flicking movement in the shadows, but thought it was only a wandering goat since there were dozens all over the place. It had been a long time since anyone had tried to enter McAdams' compound. Long ago the guards had settled into an easy existence. There had not been enough trouble to keep them on constant alert. Though when the old man was about they did to all appearances become eager guard dogs themselves, then relaxed once he was out of sight.

They knew their presence was more of a preventive measure than anything else, to insure the planter's privacy which he was rich enough to afford. McAdams had plantations on half a dozen islands and was wealthy enough to afford damn near anything he wanted.

The dog's half attempt to alert them did make them stand a bit straighter than usual and open their eyes a touch more. After all someone could try to get McAdams. True there was as much money to be made in piracy as there was in robbery but not everyone was designed for a life at sea. And rich men always made enemies along the way. There were some who would have liked to see McAdams dead or permanently out of the way.

The thought began to worry the first guard a bit.

"Thought I saw something," he muttered to his companion. "You see anything?"

"No. A damned goat most likely."

But he too searched the shadows with his eyes.

But it was a bit too late by then. The trespasser was already over the wall and hidden in the shadows.

He was not a tall man, only medium sized, with the thick square body of one who knew the ways of the dark and of close battle. Taking advantage of the tree beside the wall, he looked up into its spreading branches. The guards turned back to their dull routine of circling the grounds. As they turned the corner of the house their uninvited guest was well up into the branches groping for the white painted railing of the balcony.

The rest was child's play. By the time of half-light he was inside the bungalow and in McAdams' bedroom. Pulling the mosquito netting aside, he laid the point of the Spanish *Main Gauche* to the throat of the sleeping Scotsman.

On his face a half-smile wrinkled the scar running from his eye to the corner of his mouth.

"Wake up, McAdams. You sent for me. Remember?"

McAdams stirred, then his eyes jerked open. His first efforts to rise from his bed were quickly terminated by the point of the narrow-bladed dagger pressing against the tender flesh covering his carotid artery.

He sunk back deep into his bed. Body rigid, he forced his eyes to focus on the dark figure above him.

The face smiling at him in the thin light brought a cold feeling deep inside his bowels, and not because it was necessarily evil. No, it was the face of a man in the prime of life—somewhere in his thirties. If it hadn't been for the scar he probably would have been a most pleasant looking fellow.

"You sent for me," the man repeated. "What is it you want?"

"Laddie, I'll talk to no mon who puts steel to my throat."

Casca, the intruder, grinned approvingly and pulled the dagger back, keeping it in his hand instead of returning it to its sheath beneath his jerkin. Pulling the netting further open he bowed mockingly, "Aye. But I'd be obliged to you, good sir, if you would keep your hands in sight when you leave your bed. I have no desire to find a pistol ball lodged in my own throat." He watched McAdams' eyes. English was still a slightly strange tongue for Casca, and the flowery use of it currently in vogue didn't help matters. He hoped he sounded like the man McAdams had sent for.

Holding up both hands, the Scotsman smiled and began to wriggle out of his tousled bed. He was not as old as Casca had expected, though the full beard made age a little difficult to judge. Probably in his late fifties. He thought the man would have been older to have amassed all the wealth he was rumored to have. Especially since he had been brought to the colony as a bonded servant, little better if any than the blackest African who chopped cane in his fields.

He had a hard look to his eyes with a touch of humor behind them. Casca thought he could like this tough Scotsman who clawed his way up from the fields to be one of the richest men in the Islands. It took nerve not to be intimidated by the point of a dagger against your throat.

McAdams glanced ruefully at the open window. He

spoke quietly, almost all of the Scottish burr gone from his voice, "The guards? Did you bribe them? Or shall I have to dismiss them for their negligence?"

"Neither," Casca answered. "I just happen to be fairly good at what I do."

He meant the boast to be sarcastic, but McAdams' eyes whipped toward him, probing. That too pleased Casca. It was good to know that this man would take nothing at face value.

"Your name!"

The Scotsman barked the words as though he were the one in possession of the dagger.

"You sent for me. You ought to know who I am."

"I sent for a man called Cass Long who was foolish enough to kill the wrong person in a tavern brawl. It was the Inn of the Caribs in Montego Bay."

"I'm called Cass Long."

"But it's not your true name?"

Casca smiled. He was tempted to tell the Scotsman: "You want to know who I really am—Casca Rufio Longinus, born nearly seventeen and a half centuries past in the Rome of the Caesars." No, Scotsman, you don't want to know my name. Speaking aloud softly:

"One name will serve as well as another. It doesn't change the man."

McAdams nodded his head in silent agreement. "Now about this man you killed in Montego Bay . . ." He let the question trail off and waited.

Now that was a bit embarrassing. Casca had killed many in his time. He had few regrets about that. But the one at the inn was in truth an accident. The drunken bastard had actually killed himself and fallen on Casca's dagger. But no point in trying to prove that. And since the victim had been from an important family,

Casca had simply gotten his ass out of town and headed up to the hills where the Maroons lived. He had lain in hiding there for the last week trying to figure out a way off the island when he had gotten word from an escaped slave with family in the Scotsman's service that the master wanted to see him on a matter of business and travel.

McAdams let the sentence hang in the air as his eyes probed Casca's. "Have you any idea why I wished you to come to me?"

"No."

"Have you ever heard of Blackbeard?"

"Aye, who hasn't?"

"Stede Bonnet? Charles Vane? Israel Hands? Vauhgn, Moody, Richards, Tarleton Duncan?"

"Pirates all, aren't they?"

"Have you met any of these men I named?"

Casca shook his head, "No, I have not been long in these climes. I know none of them."

McAdams smiled inwardly with satisfaction. "Good, very good. I need a man who isn't known by these cutthroats, a man who can handle himself around them. I want something returned to me that one of them has in his possession. I'll pay 500 pounds sterling. On delivery."

"What do you want returned?"

"A girl. Tarleton Duncan, one of the captains of the coast, took her off a French ship he seized. He has her now as a hostage on his ship, the *Scorpion*."

Casca said nothing. Only his eyes showed his unspoken questions.

McAdams spoke brusquely: "That's a problem for you?"

"You want a girl who's being held captive on a pirate ship?"

"Aye."

"Well . . ."

McAdams laughed bitterly. "I know what you're thinking. Ordinarily that would be true. But Tarleton is a bit different."

"A faggot?"

McAdams snorted. "Not likely! He has the appetite of a bull at stud."

"Then . . ."

"There's something between Duncan and myself. Know only that he will not ransom her to me or I would have gladly paid. What else there is between us is only of concern to myself and no other!"

Casca eyed his host standing there in a red silk night shirt, graying hair and thick mutton whiskers alongside fleshy but determined jowls.

"So, you want me to take a girl away from Tarleton and bring her to you. It does seem a bit strange that you would trust such a task to a man you know nothing about."

"Ah . . . But you are not a simple seaman, Master Long. You were a paying passenger on the *Indian Princess*. Velvet jacket, feather in your cap, silver buckles on your shoes."

"You know what ship I came on?"

"Aye, she sailed yesterday. Too bad you ran for the hills instead of stowing away on her. You'd be on your way and far at sea by now. In addition to my plantations I also have a share in the *Indian Princess*. Therefore her master was most obliging when I asked him about you. You paid well and in gold to be brought to these far shores and the master of the *Indian Princess* performed his task well and did not inform the authorities in London that you were on board. Most fortunate for one again sought for the deaths of three of His Majesty's household guardsmen. As it is well known, the king prided himself on the martial abilities of his personal guard. It stands to reckon that one who could dispose of three of them must know how to take care of himself in dire circumstances.

Casca again cursed his luck which seemed to go from bad to worse where women and liquor were in attendance. So be it!

And like most realists, he knew when he was fairly caught. . . .

"This girl you want—"

"Michelle LeBeau. A relative. As you probably know, often in history we Scots have found France a convenient refuge during our endless wars with the masters of England. The girl is French, but her mother was my half sister."

Casca scanned him appraisingly. Except for that one moment when he had awakened, McAdams had no real Scottish accent. Well, maybe he lived in Jamaica so long that . . . Still, a small alarm bell rang in the depths of Casca's brain. Was McAdams all that he seemed to be?

"You're a rich man," Casca said. "An extremely rich man. I heard of you even in the short time I spent in Montego Bay before heading for the hills. Why do you need me to take this girl away from the pirate Duncan?"

McAdams sighed. "The trouble with dealing with an intelligent man is that you have to tell him too much.

How much do you know about freebooters?''

"Damn little.''

''There have been pirates ever since there have been ships at sea. Piracy is a business, a very, very profitable business—not just for those who practice the trade, but for businessmen too. Businessmen here in the islands. Businessmen on the coasts of the Americas. Even an American colonial governor or two has had or does have his finger in the pot. And as with many businesses—piracy flourishes during times of stress, religious or political. Now, consider Jamaica, Master Long. The Caribbean is swarming with freebooters. There is competition with Spain for control of these waters and the rich lands on which they break. At the same time the working conditions of the average laborer—whoever and whatever he may be—are such that he is no better off than an outright slave. This I know. So for those with the courage and the few with brains, signing the articles of a pirate captain presents him with a much greater opportunity than swinging a cane knife and waiting out the time of his indenturement. Have you heard of St. Mary's?''

"St. Mary's?''

''Aye, it was a pirate kingdom. A small island to the east of Madagascar where a generation ago the buccaneers had their own country. The Red Sea Men, they were called. They became fabulously wealthy preying on the Moslem ships in the Red Sea. Now right here in the Islands there is the chance for the same thing to occur, but on a much grander scale. A pirate kingdom not just on one little island, but taking in the whole region—Hispaniola, the Antilles, Honduras, Jamaica—the entire region. Can you imagine what that would mean? Whoever controls this area is master over all the southern passages to North and South America.''

McAdams turned to the table beside his bed where a carafe of red wine and crystal glasses waited.

''Wine?''

Something bothered Casca, something he could not quite put his finger on.

''But—''

McAdams smiled and handed him one of the glasses. ''I know. You don't think men who make their living raiding and butchering are smart enough to be empire builders. Well, you're right—almost. Duncan Tarleton is. He's smart enough. There is one problem though.''

Casca had not been going to say any such thing, for he had seen the same types of men rise to power time and again over the centuries, but he let McAdams continue. Responding to the last flow of the Scot's words, he asked, ''What?''

Something came into McAdams' eyes that should have warned him. But at that moment McAdams choked on his wine. The sound of his choking masked the thin sound of sandaled feet behind him.

Before Casca could register it, there was a thin cord around his neck tightening, and a very sharp point of steel in the small of his back. There was also an odd odor in the room, one Casca seemed to remember as a taste from long, long ago.

CHAPTER TWO

"Drop your weapon!" McAdams barked.

Casca did as he was bade, letting the *Main Gauche* fall from his fingers along with the wine glass.

"You didn't think you could get away with making a fool of me, did you?" McAdams asked curtly.

Casca said nothing. The cord around his neck was just tight enough to keep his vocal cords from responding. Let McAdams talk. He was listening to the breathing behind him, his nose sorting out the smells. He thought he had it about right. His eyes straight ahead he stared at McAdams, who had a good-humored look on his face.

Without warning he smashed the back of his head straight back, crushing the cartilage of the nose of the man who held the ends of the garrote about his neck. Before a grunt of pain could come from the full-fleshed lips, he had grabbed a hold on one wrist and was pivoting down and to his right side, his right leg serving as a lever that the strangler was drawn over with enough force that his grip on the garrote broke and he left the floor of the bedroom as his body twisted in the

11

air. The sound of his back hitting the hardwood floors was accompanied by the booming exhalation of air from the slave's lungs. Casca did not stop his turn. Coming up low, he blocked the oncoming thrust of the taller slave's knife and not wanting to get fancy simply grabbed a large handful of balls and applied all the pressure he could with his fingers for the space of two seconds. It was enough. The taller of the blacks hit the deck, his hands coddling his abused testicles. Casca made one further move and that was to stomp on the neck of the one who had held the garrote. The sound of his spine breaking was quite clear. Sweeping back to the floor he recovered his dagger and began to face toward McAdams who had simply stood there all this time, his wine glass still in his hand as if none of this really concerned him very much.

Before he completed his turn a shadow moved slightly in the doorway. Whipping around to face what he thought would be a new attack, he saw instead a giant white man. He lowered himself into the knife fighter's stance, left leg extended, knees bent, the right hand holding the dagger close to the side of his right leg, his left hand extended, fingers spread. The huge man in the doorway made no move one way or the other. For the space of several heartbeats it was very still in the room.

Then McAdams laughed heartily.

His voice held ungrudging admiration.

''Well, damn my eyes! You are rather good.'' He motioned to the white man who grabbed each of the slaves, the dead one and the one who still sobbed in great gasping breaths as he held onto his nearly jellied balls. He lifted them from the floor and dragged them out of the room, closing the door behind him.

Casca was a bit pissed off.

"You set that up for some kind of a show?"

"No, no. They were just coming to waken me. Planters do rise early you know."

"What about the choking on the wine?"

McAdams snorted amusedly at his little joke, "Well, yes. There was this opportunity to see how you handled yourself in unexpected situations."

Casca's face turned hard. He had killed a man for no reason.

McAdams snorted again at the hardness he saw gathering around the eyes and mouth of his guest. "Very well then. I'll make it an even thousand pounds and guarantee you passage to anywhere you may wish to go after completing the job."

"That's a lot of money for one woman, even a niece."

"I have a lot of money. Besides . . ."

"Besides what?"

"You might have a little difficulty with Tarleton Duncan." Again his eyes probed Casca's. "I would not be displeased if you were to kill him."

McAdams had dressed and Casca was sitting with him on an open veranda eating breakfast. The sun was up. It lay like a dust of thin gold over the tops of the emerald forest that stretched out below them. Gold. There were times when Casca wondered why the hell men were so anxious to acquire the stuff. Too much of it seemed to make its owners all a little mad.

"Try some of this," McAdams urged, offering Casca a dish of a sticky white substance. Casca tasted it, wanted to spit it out, but didn't. McAdams laughed at him.

"What is it?"

McAdams spooned a large portion into his mouth and smacked his lips. "You have to acquire a taste for it as I did when I was a bonded man. It's called 'acky' ''—which to Casca was what it tasted like. McAdams pointed out a tall tree with wide spreading branches, saying that that was where the stuff came from, but when Casca looked, he saw beyond the tree on the far horizon the topsails of a ship, golden in the morning sun.

"Probably Mr. Teach, better known as, as I said earlier, Blackbeard," McAdams observed. "He's coming in today. We'll get you aboard."

Casca looked at him. Pirates coming and going on schedule? What was McAdams up to? What was his real reason for wanting the girl?

"We'll have to get you some clothes," McAdams said, reaching for a small silver bell on the table.

"Get me aboard?" Casca queried. "How are you going to do that?"

"Oh, I have some influence with the good captain as well as with some members of Duncan's crew." He rose from the table.

Well if you have men there, what do you need me for? Casca thought. He was beginning to have his doubts about this, but there wasn't much he could do about it. This seemed to be the only path to take right now that could get him off the island quickly. He followed McAdams and the servant who had answered the silver bell. Half an hour later he was dressed in what surely must be the height of fashion in London—or more likely Paris: justacorps, dark blue waistcoat, short breeches, elegant stockings, and the

most expensive mahogany colored boots he had seen
for a long time.

"Why so elaborate?"

"Blackbeard has a reputation of which he is proud,
but he is still a fool in many ways, impressed by quality
folk. It will please his ego to have a gentleman in his
company. Therefore we shall make you one, Master
Long. You are now Squire Long, a man of quality who
has fallen upon evil times and is forced to seek refuge
where he may find it." He handed Casca a brace of
pistols hung on a silk sash and a small sword with a
silver engraved hanger.

At the door of the waiting carriage, McAdams even
shook his hand and wished him luck. Bring back my
niece to me for I value her highly and am responsible
for her well-being. As long as Duncan has her he can
force her to do his bidding. I have chosen you for my
agent because you are unknown and you appear to have
the skills I require. I will gamble on you, Cass Long.
But remember, I am not a good loser."

It sounded simple enough. McAdams had made
arrangements to get Casca properly introduced to one
of the leaders of the freebooters community and from
there all he had to do was get on board Tarleton's ship,
the *Scorpion*, rescue the French girl and bring her back
to her uncle. He would then collect his money and be
gone.

Opening the door of the carriage, he climbed in and
looked casually at the man McAdams had waiting to
take him to Blackbeard's crew, the man who was to be
his contact. That was when he almost broke off the
whole thing. Inside was the giant white man who had
been in the doorway of McAdams' bedroom.

"Let me introduce you," McAdams said. "This is Big Jim, who some call, for an unknown reason, the Dutchman. He saw your show at the Carib, in whose establishment, by the way, I am also a small partner."

A child's voice, crying happily, "Daddy, Daddy!" in the morning sun was just about the last straw for Casca. Looking out the window of the carriage he saw a little boy of not over four or five years of age running toward McAdams. Behind him came a woman obviously pregnant and most certainly the child's mother.

McAdams presented a perfect picture of the kind of wealthy self-made man who loved his family and tried to do his best by them.

Casca also knew that McAdams had a touch of ruthlessness to him as demonstrated by the senseless death of one of his slaves for whom he'd shown no more concern than if the man had been cockroach. As the carriage jolted away he wondered if the reason McAdams wanted his niece back was true. He didn't seem like the kind of man who could be blackmailed very easily, but then where things of family and blood were concerned logic was not always the rule.

His companion, Big Jim, said nothing. He merely looked blankly out the window as they began the ride down the mountainside to where the air was thick and hot leaving the cooler climes of the high ground behind them.

Casca watched the giant's face, but the man said nothing. He just rode quietly with the smile of a child on his face.

But he smelled.

Casca recalled now where he'd first smelled that strange odor, that strange heavy "brownness." It was in the Eagle's Nest of Hassan al Sabah in Persia. Hashish.

At any rate it was none of his business. Casca had no desire to either reform or corrupt the world around him. But if Big Jim was to be his contact with McAdams, he would be spending a bit of time with him so he tried to strike up a conversation.

He got nowhere. The giant seemed to have a perpetual grin on his face, but he spoke no words. Casca wondered why he was called Big Jim. Maybe it was because that was what he looked like. He had thick heavy shoulders and blondish red fuzz on a square head set on an even thicker square neck. The full face had rosy cheeks and a small pursed mouth which looked as though it would have been better set in the face of a child.

They had been jolting downward for nearly half an hour when it suddenly dawned on Casca why the giant didn't talk very much.

The big bastard wasn't carrying a full complement of guns. He was simpleminded.

And this was going to be his ticket to the world of the freebooters.

Settling back in the soft cushions of the jolting carriage he decided there was only one way to describe this day.

Bullshit!

What he didn't know was that about a quarter of a mile down the mountainside, in an exceptionally thick forested part of the mountain, the road narrowed and made a sharp and difficult turn—a perfect ambush site.

Waiting in ambush were a dozen escaped slaves,

Maroons, men who had more than enough cause to hate the rich who rode in carriages, and were willing to do something about it. They heard the clatter of the wheels and prepared themselves.

CHAPTER THREE

The rhythmic motion of the carriage lulled Casca. The morning sun, coming through the open carriage window, warmed his face. Drowsiness crept into his eyes; it had been a long night.

He felt calm and comfortable. Nothing bothered him, not even the silent grinning giant on the seat beside him. He thought of a time long past when he had been much richer than old McAdams could have ever dreamed of. The thought brought a smile to his lips. The dim-witted giant with him saw the smile and grinned even wider.

Casca thought, he must think I'm as barmy as he is. Looking out the window he could see the path the carriage took. The road ran down beside a small gorge, and the gorge was on his side of the carriage. He couldn't see ahead though. For a moment that fact vaguely bothered him, for he had idly noted that the cover was getting denser, the trees closer together and the underbrush much thicker. It was a good place for an ambush. Wonder what's ahead? Now, that was a stupid thing to be worrying about. I've been in too

many battles, he told himself. Now I'm seeing trouble
in the middle of paradise. And the Blue Mountains of
Jamaica were as close to paradise as he was likely to get
on this earth. The morning was now clear, the air
moving with the sea breeze as light as crystal. Every
detail—the green branches of the trees, the lush colors
of tropical flowers growing in wild profusion beside
the trail, the outcroppings of rock—was sharply cut
and distinct. And now they were approaching a small
waterfall formed by a delicate stream of the purest
water, splashing across the brown rocks, the spray
turned rainbow colors in the sun. By the gods, it was
pretty and so peaceful. He wished fleetingly, knowing
it was impossible, that he could find somewhere on the
earth where he could sit and be at peace, letting the
seasons turn in their endless course till at last he too
passed on. Sometimes he felt so old, so tired. . . . He
shook his head to rid it of the cobwebs which were
becoming too thick. He was thinking too much. And
that was dangerous. The few times in his existence
he'd done too much thinking he had wound up with his
ass in a sling. He was still contemplating the troubles
that too much thought had gotten him into when the
first arrow from the Maroon bowmen cut through the
carriage window—within inches of his face.

It buried its steel point in the wooden framework of
the opposite side of the coach, the feathered nock end
momentarily quivering in a blur of red and brown.

The Maroon leader was an exceptionally tall black
man—nearly seven feet—and had muscles that came
from a hundred generations of ancestors who lived on
the plains and deserts of an environment that knew no
mercy. He was stripped to the waist. His body had no

visible sign of hair on it, which accented the long tough sinews of his chest muscles even more. Scars covered his face and arms and back. Not all of them were tribal markings. Most had come from the *kiboko*, rhinoceros hide whips used by the Arab slavers who had taken him captive and brought him to his new masters in these strange and distant lands. He had the thin facial features of one with some Masai blood with dark intelligent eyes that observed the carriage as it careened to a halt to avoid the log he had placed across the trail. At what he judged to be the right moment, he yelled—not really a word or a command, but a single, high-pitched cry like that of a night bird.

He had planned his ambush well. This was the spot where the road narrowed and deepened showing the sea across the dropping land. Anyone driving here would have to come to an almost complete stop to negotiate the sharp turn. He placed the log so that the carriage would have to stop in order to avoid going off the side of the gorge. He wanted McAdams alive. But he had no idea McAdams wasn't in the carriage. That was his fatal mistake.

The first flight of arrows from his bowmen in the trees killed the driver. The archers comprised all the firepower the Maroon leader had. Neither he nor the half-dozen men with him had any weapons other than clubs and knives. He did not expect too much trouble from the passengers. The carriage was small and if he moved quickly he would have the advantage of surprise and numbers on his side. At the leader's cry his men converged upon the stationary carriage.

Casca could see none of this. He heard the Maroon leader's cry as they lurched to a sudden stop, the horses trying to avoid having their legs broken by the log barrier. From the jungle he heard the sounds of men coming to the side of the carriage where his silent giant companion sat. But Casca had been in ambushes before. He sat perfectly still. And out of his side vision he could see that the giant was doing the same thing. Good. He was an old pro, then. Slow, maybe, but that need not affect how he fought.

While this was going through Casca's mind there was a noise on the roof of the carriage, and a moment later the body of the driver fell past Casca's open window.

At the same time, the Maroons had reached the giant's side of the carriage, and two of them now pulled the door open.

One of them was a skinny young fellow, not much past boyhood. The other was about Casca's size and weight and in his late thirties. Both had Gullah features. They might have been brothers.

The giant moved.

One moment he was sitting motionless on the carriage seat. The next, he had the younger Maroon's neck in one powerful arm and was pushing him backward into the second Gullah, and then came the sharp crack of the boy's breaking neck!

Casca followed them, right hand on his sword, eyes alert for any who might have guns.

When he saw that none of the Maroons had weapons other than clubs, the deep sadness and the rage within him boiled together, and he pulled his sword from its hanger and slashed out to get this over with as quickly as possible. By now he knew who the attackers were, knew that they were poor, hungry fugitives. In his mind he silently cursed a world where he could come from a rich man's breakfast table, from a man who had everything, to men who had nothing; all this in less than a quarter hour. He felt a great pity for these Maroons.

But, pity or not, they were out to kill him. It was kill or be killed. He had the sword, and he used it.

Finally, it was he and the Maroon leader. The giant was finishing off the last of the others. The Maroon leader was fairly good with the club—and with his nearly seven feet of height and long arms he had the reach on Casca. He fought well, blocking Casca's cuts with his club, parrying his thrusts.

Casca stepped back. "You fight well. Want to call a draw of it?"

A shadow passed across the face of the leader, and for a moment he seemed to waver in indecision. Then he drew back his club and rushed Casca.

"I'm sorry," Casca said and pushed the sword into the chest wall, into the heart, a quick, familiar move with his own body turned inside the oncoming club. The Maroon was dead before he had finished his rush.

Casca pulled the blade from the fallen body, watching the blood drip off the edge onto the hairless chest of the Maroon.

"I'm sorry," he repeated softly to the dead man. He really was. He hadn't wanted to kill any of these men.

"Watch!"

The giant's cry broke the spell for Casca, and he whirled just in time for an arrow to miss him. But he had seen the movement in the trees across the gorge where the archers were hidden, and he instinctively pulled one of the pistols from his sash, aimed carefully and fired.

The gun roared in the morning air, the gorge picking

up the sound and amplifying it. There was a high-pitched cry from the tree, and then a body fell from the branches, still clutching a makeshift bow.

The body fell on an outcropping of the brown rock just under the trees, seemed to bounce once, then tilted and slowly began to slide down into the gorge. There was plenty of time for Casca to see it quite clearly, to see the face of the dead one.

A woman.

The Maroon leader had put his women into the trees with makeshift bows and arrows.

Casca looked out across the forest top to the distant sea where the sails of ships—pirate ships—were blowing in from the horizon.

The morning was no longer beautiful.

CHAPTER FOUR

What the hell?

Casca was sitting in the rear of a small boat being rowed out to Blackbeard's ship. The giant Dutchman sat facing him, a silly grin twisting his round cheeks so it appeared his blue eyes were resting on top of two squashed apples. He looked laughable, but in the mood Casca was in nothing was amusing.

But it wasn't the Dutchman that had Casca's attention.

It was the ship itself.

Smoke poured out of the portholes of the deckhouse, heavy, dark smoke that streamed sullenly over the aft end of the ship. As they got closer, Casca could smell the sulfurous fumes, and he began to wonder where the powder magazine was on the vessel. Something was burning—that was for damn sure.

Yet the little pirate manning the oars didn't seem to care. He was a scrawny, small bastard with a weasel face, and he didn't look like he was big enough to lift one oar, much less to scull the boat over the water as rapidly as he was now doing. But Casca thought he saw intelligence in the quick-moving eyes—certainly a hell of a lot more intelligence than in the face of the big Dutchman. So he asked about the fire on Blackbeard's ship.

"What the hell is all the smoke for?" he growled at the oarsman.

The little pirate grinned. "Cap'n's got all the officers below decks. Swears he can stand the brimstone forever, since he's the Devil himself."

"What?"

"That's the Cap'n for you. He'll do it, too. Wait a little mite, and them fellows'll be stumbling out the hatch a-choking. Then here'll come the Cap'n, laughing like hell."

The big Dutchman nodded his head in agreement, grinning.

Shit! Casca thought. Now I've got myself involved with a bunch of damned madmen.

For the hundredth time he cursed his stupidity in going ashore at Montego Bay and killing that son of a bitch. If he had stayed on the ship, he'd be halfway to Charles Town by now. And since he was mad at himself, he was also mad at the whole damned world. The urge to kick somebody's ass was strong in him, and he even glowered at the giant Dutchman, the closest person to him. The stupid giant only grinned back.

Damn!

Even the ship didn't give Casca any excuse to vent the wrath building in him. The brig was well-founded. She had good lines and looked like she'd be a good sailor—that is, as far as Casca could tell. Even after all the years he had lived he was still not as comfortable on water as on land.

"Now, ain't you a pretty sight?"

The fat pirate who met Casca as he climbed up the ship's ladder and came aboard didn't know what he was getting himself into. He was big, mean, and strong, a mixed-race hulk of a man naked to the waist, with big, ham hands and small, cruel eyes. He was very drunk, and in addition, all the ship's officers were below decks with the captain, so the sight of the elegantly dressed Casca signaled fair game to him.

Casca had looked around the deck when he came aboard, and the slow match of his anger was becoming a short fuse. The ship's deck was incredibly filthy. Even as Casca came aboard one of the crewmen was taking a shit in the scuppers. Another had just finished a bottle, and instead of throwing the empty over the side, had deliberately thrown it at the mast where it broke, spreading shards of glass on the dirty deck. All the crewmen in sight were obviously drunk. How they could have handled the ship so smartly just a little while ago was a mystery to Casca. But what wasn't a mystery was the mess on deck. Give him five minutes with these bastards and he'd have them off their asses and cleaning things up. It was not that Casca was squeamish. Hell, he'd spent his share of the time in battle—and in a lot of unpleasant places. But, dammit, his training had made him revolt at anything that kept a fighting machine from battle readiness.

But the fat pirate didn't know any of that. All he saw was a dandy—somebody he could have some fun with.

When Casca ignored him, he waddled forward, eyes dark.

"Hey, pretty boy, I'm talking to you."

Casca sighed, looked forward momentarily to taking out his bad humor on the fat man, then thought better of it. After all, what happened on Blackbeard's ship was none of his business. What he wanted to do was carry out McAdams' project, and get the girl—and then get on to America. Damn the interruptions. Frowning at the drunk pirate, he reached into the leather purse hanging at his waist, intending to pull out a piece of eight. His fingers brought out two. Casca threw one down on the deck in front of the pirate. "Go ashore and buy yourself a bath," he said, turning toward the hatch. He still had the other piece of eight in his right hand.

"Hey!"

Several things happened at once.

The fat pirate was mad now, and drew the cutlass he carried around his waist out of its sheath. At the same time, the aft hatch cover was pushed violently open, and the officers of the ship, coughing and cursing, burst out into the sunlight. With them a thick pall of sulfurous smoke boiled up.

There was something else, too, something in the open hatch that caught Casca's eye—but he was too busy at the moment to pay attention to it.

The fat pirate lunged toward him, swinging the cutlass, no longer interested in just making fun of Casca. Right now he was making a tremendous slash, intending to chop Casca right down the middle.

As for Casca, he was caught off guard, his attention finally drawn toward the opening hatch, never dreaming the fat pirate was really drunk enough to come at him.

So the steel flashed in the sunlight, aimed straight for his skull, and when Casca tried to dodge it, his left foot slipped in some filth on the deck, throwing his body directly toward the pirate.

Damn!

The cutting edge of the cutlass was not not much more than a foot from his head, too close to avoid, so Casca continued his forward fall, using the purchase of his right foot to aid his lunge, and balling up his right fist.

The punch he threw had all his weight and force behind it, and it landed exactly where he aimed; at the fat pirate's nuts.

The pirate was still driving forward, and the momentum of his rush coupled with the force of his cutlass blow and the lowered target of Casca's bent-over body rolled him up into the air, big and fat as he was, and he slammed into the bulwark, head first, body tilted down, screaming with pain from the blow to his genitals.

Casca was pissed off for having to slug the fat bastard's nuts with his naked fist, so now he used his booted right foot to repeat the blow. At the same time he grabbed the pirate's cutlass hand and jerked it backwards so hard that there was a crack of breaking bone before the pirate dropped the weapon. And, to add insult to injury, Casca continued his swing and then pushed. The pirate was already off balance. He was teetering on the rim of the bulwark. Now Casca's push flipped him all the way over, and slowly at first, then with speed, he described a rough cartwheel in the air and dropped toward the ocean.

Casca stepped back to avoid the falling cutlass, then spat over the bulwark. He was red in the face, more with anger than with the exertion.

"Well, damn my eyes!"

The sound of the voice came as a shock. It came to Casca then that the events of the last few seconds had happened in total silence except for the sounds of his scuffle with the fat pirate and the pirate's screams. Now he turned toward the opened hatch—just as the falling pirate's body splashed into the water.

"Thou art one fine son of a bitch of a fighter!"

The booming voice came from the apparition that was emerging from the smoking hatch: an obviously very big, bearded man with laughing eyes that seemed larger than they were. But what made him seem so strange was the fact that the beard had been allowed to grow very long, and various ends of it were plaited together around burning strips of slow match, so his face was wreathed in dirty hair, glowing embers, fire, and smoke.

Blackbeard the pirate.

And it was obvious that he had taken a liking to Casca.

Ordinarily Casca was not one to take a disliking to anyone at first glance. He had been a soldier too long. His philosophy was live and let live.

Blackbeard the pirate was an exception.

Casca knew from the moment he saw the man that he would thoroughly dislike Blackbeard. There was just something about a man who plaited slow match into his whiskers.

Still . . .

It was really none of Casca's business. Blackbeard was just a carriage driver to get him where he was going.

"Aye, lad, thou art worthy to serve under Captain Teach. Hast thou come to join my crew?" Blackbeard had come up to Casca now. And he was a big man.

Before Casca could answer him, the Dutchman, Big Jim pulled a sealed letter from within his shirt and handed it to Blackbeard, grinning sillily, but saying nothing.

Blackbeard broke the wax seal, unfolded the document and read, slowly and silently. When he finished, he looked at Casca a little disappointed.

"Duncan Tarleton, eh? Why, damn my eyes, Squire Cass Long, what else can you do besides fight?"

Blackbeard stunk. Maybe it was just the slow match. Maybe something else. Or maybe Casca had already decided nothing would make him like the bastard. An idea formed in his mind. His own particular sense of humor.

"I can find money in the damndest places," he answered, reaching up toward Blackbeard's beard. He still had the second piece of eight in his hand, and he palmed it as he reached up, and apparently plucked it from the tiny flame of one of the slow matches. "Like this." He held the coin in front of Blackbeard between his fingers, turning it slowly.

Blackbeard took the coin, examined it carefully, then looked searchingly at Casca.

"Well, damn my eyes!"

It wasn't much of a trick. Casca had picked up the technique from a renegade Italian magician nearly five hundred years before. And after he had done it, he wasn't sure it had been a good idea.

Blackbeard was looking at him with an expression in his dark eyes that Casca couldn't read.

Had he impressed the pirate?

Or had he just made an enemy of him?

CHAPTER FIVE

McAdams watched the sails of Blackbeard's ship head out to the blue water and nodded his head in satisfaction. Whether or not the man he had sent to Blackbeard for transport could do the job or not was in the hands of the gods. Yet he was content. One thing he knew from their short meeting together: wherever Cass Long went there would be trouble. And that was what he wished for Tarleton. Trouble to make up for what had been done to him. The girl was just the icing on the cake. This Cass Long was just the beginning of the trouble he planned for Tarleton. The dog would learn soon enough who his master was. Unless of course Squire Long put an end to the man—a permanent end.

The brig stood out to sea. The shoreline of Jamaica, with the softened ridge of central mountains beyond, slipped into the haze behind them. Casca, who had nothing to do for now save let the sea miles slide by, stood at the taffrail, listening to the foaming bubbles of the sea slipping past the stern of the ship.

He had company, the second mate of one of

Blackbeard's subordinate captains. Casca had not caught the name, and really didn't care since it was no concern of his. The only good thing he could say about the man was that he was unusually clean for one of his ilk, and wore more sedate and refined clothing: a white shirt open at the throat, sleeves rolled up past the elbows and dark blue breeches with plain three-quarter boots. From his shoulders hung the inevitable brace of pistol, and a blade larger than a dirk but smaller than a short sword sat in a sheath at his waist. They were plain, efficient tools made for use, not show. He was about Casca's height and build, could have almost passed as a relative except for his excessively blond hair and deep blue eyes. There was also a look about his face that was different from Casca's. He was, in short, very much out of place on this pirate vessel, and Casca had briefly considered the oddity of such a ''gentlemen'' Blackbeard had introduced him to Casca as ''another one of your damned gentlemen'' being the mate of a pirate ship. But only briefly. Casca really didn't care. The sooner he got to Charles Town and America the better. Still, there was one thing he liked about the mate—aside from the fact that he didn't stink—he didn't talk much, and when he did it was the kind of talk you could go along with, like maybe he respected what you had to say and was willing to accept you.

Besides, he had the look of a damn good fighter.

''Beautiful little island. Bloody beautiful.'' He was puffing on a long clay pipe—a Dutch clay, Casca decided, though he was not really an expert on tobacco smoking—which he had tamped full while standing beside Casca.

He wants to find out something from me, Casca

thought, not taken in at all by the mate's elaborately casual manner.

Well, that was all right. He ought to be finding out something about Tarleton Duncan. Only thing was, Casca felt lazy. He wasn't really interested in working right now.

"You've been up in those mountains, haven't you?" The mate used the pipe as a pointer, aiming at Jamaica's Blue Mountains now on the horizon.

Casca nodded.

"Ever known McAdams before?"

Casca shook his head.

"Richest man in the Caribbean. Bit of a mystery how he got started. Bit of a mystery, that." He puffed briefly on the pipe. "Understand you're a squire. You don't look English. You look Italian."

"One of my ancestors did a favor for King Richard during the Crusades," Casca lied. "The king was properly grateful. Gave a little land."

"You don't sound English when you talk, either," the mate said. "But, no matter. In our line of work, not good form to pry too closely into the past. Not good form at all." He took a long drag at the pipe. "The future, now that's a different matter. Understand you're going with Tarleton Duncan."

Casca nodded.

"Now, there's a queer one. All kinds of stories about that one."

"Such as?"

"Ah! Friend Cass Long, you'll be sailing with the man. 'Tis not for me to say."

"Good reputation? Or bad?"

"Depends on who you are."

"Does he know his craft?"

"Aye! That he does. More than enough to keep Teach worried."

"Teach?"

"Teach. Blackbeard. This ship's captain, he of the slow match posies in his beard."

"I take it you don't approve."

"Friend Long, I neither approve nor disapprove of what's none of my business."

"Why should Blackbeard be worried?"

"Because when you're the leader, there's always somebody under you who wants to take over."

"And you think Duncan will?" It was not likely that Tarleton Duncan would get the chance, Casca thought grimly. Not if he were successful in what he had contracted with McAdams to do. Still . . . Something bothered Casca, something in the back of his mind that he couldn't quite grab a hold of. He wasn't too sure he really wanted to kill this Tarleton Duncan he had never seen and deliver the woman to McAdams. The whole deal smelled. There was just something wrong with it. He should let McAdams do his own dirty work. Besides, Duncan could hardly be worse than Blackbeard. And as for the woman, hell! There were a lot of women in the world.

"Friend Long," the mate was answering him, "I don't think so unless there's something in it for me." The mate puffed slowly on his pipe. He seemed totally content despite the fact that not ten feet behind him two of Blackbeard's pirates had gotten into a loud argument, the kind Casca recognized as a killing argument.

Apparently Blackbeard encouraged such behavior because when Casca looked aft he saw the pirate captain grinning with glee as he watched the two argue. Stupid! Casca didn't really know why his hatred for

Blackbeard was so violent. He could give a lot of small reasons, but there was some big one that he couldn't quite put his finger on. What he did know was that he would gladly kick the shit out of the big pirate chief— and that would take some doing because even though Blackbeard was a show-off and a clown, he was also a big tub of a man. It would take a lot of cutlass swings to slash through that dirty gristle.

There was something else, too.

Casca had that same kind of restless feeling he had often known before when he was waiting out the coming of a battle. All this standing around doing nothing was getting to him. He was tempted to interfere in the brawl between the two pirates just because he was bored. To take his mind off of it, he looked out to sea. Nothing but blue deserted water under the hot sun, empty water going to meet an equally empty sky in a confused, hazy area where the two met.

"Why do you wish to join the Brotherhood?"

For a moment Casca thought of the Brotherhood of the Lamb—something he sure as hell wasn't about to join! Then he realized that the mate was talking about piracy. Before he could answer, though, the mate said: "Did you get bored? That was it with Stede Bonnet. Got tired of a nagging wife. You married, Friend Long?"

"No."

"Well, there they go." The mate pointed with the stem of his pipe at the two ships that had been with them, but were now turning away. "On their way to Charles Town."

"Charles Town!"

"Yes. Didn't you know?"

Casca swore. In Latin. To himself.

The mate was looking at him appraisingly, puzzled by his reaction. "Charles Town," he repeated. "As a matter of fact that's where we're headed—Captain Teach. My captain's ship will be there, too. That's why I'm along."

"I thought—"

"That we were going to meet Tarleton Duncan? We are. Teach will put you aboard then. Duncan and the ships with him are going to raid south. We're going up through the Straits."

"To Charles Town?"

"Charles Town." The mate looked puzzled as Casca hurried off aft toward Blackbeard.

Casca had the sudden feeling that he'd best be rid of McAdams' proposition and should go on with his original plan. As for the money, he'd never been able to hang on to it anyway.

"You do? Well, damn my eyes, Master Long, we can accommodate you. Aye, me bucko, consider yourself signed on as of this very moment." Blackbeard was still grinning. Casca's request to join his crew rather than Tarleton Duncan's had only served to spread Teach's red lips a little further apart.

But there was the shadow of a slightly shrewd look in his eyes that bothered Casca. Like perhaps he wasn't quite sure about Casca and would be watching him. That—and the flowery speech—put him on his guard.

"Aye, by damnation and perdition we'll make a proper freebooter out of ye, Master Long."

Casca groaned inwardly. Why didn't the cloying bastard just say what he had to say and leave out all the extra words? But if Blackbeard was going to Charles Town, he could put up with it for a while. He knew of course that switching crews meant he was going to suffer a loss of honor. Damn! he thought, I'm getting as bad as the people around me.

"Sail ho! Two points abaft the port bow!"

The lookout cry from the top of the mast broke into Casca's thought. Blackbeard, standing beside him, roared orders. Suddenly the brig boiled with a confused mass of men running to stations, shouting.

Casca tried to sight the vessel, but as far as he could tell she was only a shapeless mass in the confused line between sea and sky, though, as he watched, she grew rapidly larger, sails taking shape first, then the dark blob of the hull.

"What do ye make of her?" Blackbeard roared at the lookout.

No answer.

"Damn you! What is she?"

Another pause. Then, just as Casca heard Blackbeard draw in his breath for another roar, the lookout yelled:

"Spaniard! She's a damn Spaniard!"

Blackbeard roared. The mates shouted. Men ran to their stations. The brig came about. They went in for the attack.

With all sails crowded on, and having the advantage of the weather eye, the pirate brig bore down on its quarry. Casca had found himself again beside the passenger mate with whom he had been talking. Only now the mate had put up his pipe and was looking intently out at the target ship. His right hand was on the hilt of his sword. Passenger or no passenger, when it came to a fight there would apparently be no noncombatants aboard a pirate ship. It occurred to Casca that this would be his first battle as a pirate. He was not exactly looking forward to it. His opinion of his "shipmates" was not all that high, and, as for his opinion of his "commander," well . . .

"What's the standard tactic?" he asked the mate.

"Close, sweep their decks with grape, board."

"That all?"

"That's all there is to it."

Quickly they overtook the Spaniard, and when they were close, at the shouted order of the captain, they turned broadside to bring the guns to bear.

The sudden tilting of the deck made the mate beside Casca reach upward with his left hand to steady himself on the slanting deck. Casca saw the motion only casually, for he, too, had reached for the rigging. But a flash of silver on the mate's wrist instantly brought his eyes back.

On a silver chain around the mate's wrist was a half-shekel—or at least that was what he thought he saw before the mate's hand came down and the sleeve again covered the jewelry.

"Where did you get that?" he roared.

But no sooner were the words out of his mouth than the order to fire came, and the brig's starboard cannon blasted the sunlight in a ragged, but rather close, volley.

Immediately the choking smell of burnt powder and the greasy billowing of black smoke, boiled up around them, momentarily hiding both the sea and the lower part of the other ship. Casca, though, was intent only on the mate, whom he grabbed by the sleeve and again demanded: "Where did you get the coin?"

But as the mate answered, some pirate in the rigging shouted: "Look out! Damn them! They're firing back!'' And the mate's words were broken. Casca got only bits and pieces:

''. . . one . . . Tarle—''

That was all. The Spanish broadside came then, grapeshot through the black smoke, shot that whistled through rigging and cut stays and smashed into flesh and buried into timbers and bulwarks and mast.

One shot made a direct hit in the exact center of the mate's face. Casca saw the flesh explode outward like a huge upside-down red mushroom before the blood and pieces of bone sprayed over his own eyes, blinding him for the moment, as though he were covered with thick red mud.

And, at the same time, the two ships came violently together. Casca felt the mate's body torn from him by the shock, and when he had hastily wiped enough blood from his eyes to see a little, his first sight was that of the mate's arm, the one with the silver chain and coin, falling down between the two ships. They had just hit, rolled, and now, rolling back, crushed the mate's arm between them. Whatever was on that arm was now ground between the two hulls and lost forever, downward into the sea.

CHAPTER SIX

For some seconds after the two ships collided, crushing the mate's arm, Casca stood holding onto the rigging, dazed with memories. Once in a while something he saw would bring back the past to him in a rush.

The muzzle blast of a Spaniard's musket shocked him out of his reverie. While he dreamed of the past, here in the present the battle had been fairly joined. The two ships were now grappled close together, two wooden lovers, one of which would devour the other once the joining was complete.

From the deck of Blackbeard's ship the pirate boarders had leaped onto the other deck howling for blood. But the Spaniards, too, were fighting. And the musket that now caught Casca's attention, the gun that would fire in a fraction of a thought, was pointed right beside him—not at Casca himself, but at the retarded giant who had come with him from McAdams. Somehow he had ended up beside Casca and was wedged between him and a pirate on his other side. Seeing the musket held on his belly at point-blank range he realized too late that he was unable to do anything about it. The load of shot—the musket was the old-fashioned kind with a bell-shaped muzzle—would burn his gut; it would not be a happy way to die.

Coming out of his daydream, Casca saw that he had no time for thought. His right hand was already beside the belaying pin. In one swift motion he had it wrenched free, his arm back, and the pin thrown. His aim was perfect. The heavy rounded handle end of the belaying pin smashed squarely into the eye of the Spaniard holding the musket, crushing lens and iris and shocking inward toward the brain in a storm of blood and watery fluid. The instant pain was so great that the Spaniard threw up his hands at the same moment that he screamed, so that when the musket went off the pattern of shot was upward, and the deadly pieces of iron and lead shrieked just over the head of the retarded giant, almost touching the tousled hair. Had he been wearing a helmet or a hat it would have been blown off.

Casca had thrown the pin at the one instant when the two ships were momentarily motionless in regard to each other. No, as the musket fired, the waves crashed the two downward again, and the boarders still on Blackbeard's brig leaped for the deck of the Spaniard, and Casca was carried with them. He pulled his sword and got into the fight.

The first Spaniard before him was a big fat lard-tub of a man with a long greasy beard. Casca hacked with his sword, the pent-up feeling in him wanting to be released. His blade cut down the Spaniard's arm, slicing off a big hunk of fat and flesh, but there was so much fat on the Spaniard not much blood came. Casca stabbed him in the gut. The Spaniard made no noise, but then the sound of fighting around them was so heavy that it would not have made any difference anyway. When Casca jerked the sword free, he saw another Spaniard beside the fat man swinging at him with a cutlass, and he swept the now bloody sword up in an arc from the fat man and slit the Spaniard's throat. Then he got back to work on the fat man.

After that it was like any other battle he had ever fought: a confused dream of blood and cries and sharp steel . . . of men who screamed and cursed and fought, slipping in the blood on the deck, slashing with the blades, killing, dying. Only one Spaniard bothered Casca—a youngster not yet bearded. When Casca's sword went into his chest it was like cutting into the soft belly of a woman, and there was a look in the boy's eyes as he died that Casca would long remember. But the boy had had a pistol, and it had been pointed at Casca's gut. Casca pulled his sword savagely from the body of the dead youth and looked for someone he could really enjoy killing.

He found the one in a squat, beetle-browed son of a bitch who was so damn good with a cutlass that at first Casca had to work to keep alive. But then the Spaniard made the mistake of being too slow on his follow-through. Casca got his own blade within the swing and, when he slashed, did so with a quick pull of his wrist. The move neatly sliced the Spaniard's hand from his arm, and while he was looking stupidly down at the blood spouting from the stump, Casca brought his blade back in another slicing arc combined with a thrust. The Spaniard would be singing soprano if he lived because his testicles were now on the tip of Casca's sword.

What happened to him then, Casca did not know because two Spaniards were coming at him at the same time, and they were both good. But he was high on the lust for battle, charged with a feeling of invincible power, and he cut and thrust like a madman, and he had them.

It was then, as he was pulling the sword back from the second dead body, that he heard the voice behind and slightly above him:

"Watch it, Cass Long! Do too good, and you'll make Blackbeard jealous."

Casca recognized the voice—but didn't believe it. He had a Spaniard in front of him, so he had to parry that one's rapier thrust, but when he stepped aside, he could see who was behind him, who had spoken, low, into his ear.

The retarded giant!

Casca knocked the rapier from the Spaniard's grasp and brought his own blade back across the man's throat, severing the jugular, and again grabbed a quick glance at the giant. There was just the slightest upturn to the corner of his mouth, and a very faint, momentary glint in the eyes—then the man's face again took on the vacuous stare of the simpleton.

Casca thought, now why does he pretend to be stupid if he's not?

Damn! Casca ducked just in time to miss a very wicked cutlass slash. Too much thinking! Gotten him in trouble before. Would get him in trouble again. He parried the next Spanish blow and was all set to attack when the Spaniard's face blew up in a miniature volcano of blood, bone and gristle. At the same time Casca was deafened by the two simultaneous pistol shots just behind him, almost at ear level. He turned.

Israel Hands, Blackbeard's official captain, was holding the two pistols. There was an odd half-smile on his face as he said to Casca: "Captain wants to see you in his cabin after the prize is secured."

Israel Hands glanced at the Spanish ship, saw that all resistance was over, put up his pistols without reloading and limped away.

Casca watched the limp. The mate had told him earlier where Hands had gotten it. "That? Oh, one of Captain Teach's savage humors. One night he's drinking in his cabin with the pilot and with a man I don't know and with Israel Hands there. The captain, without provocation, secretly drew out a small pair of pistols and cocked them under the table. This man I don't know saw what Teach was doing and left, not telling the pilot or Hands. When the captain had the pistols ready, he blew out the candle on the table, crossed his hands, and discharged both pieces. The one aimed at Hands shot him through the knee and lamed him for life. The one aimed at the pilot missed. You know, Cass Long, what Blackbeard said when they asked him why he did it?"

"No."

"Says, 'Damn you! If I did not now and then kill one of you, you'd forget who I was.' "

Remembering that now, Casca looked forward to where Blackbeard was standing in the bow and saw that the pirate chief was watching him, evident pleasure in his eyes.

Damn! The son of a bitch is probably going to promote me. Casca saw that the pirates he passed were looking at him curiously, almost with respect. Shit! Damn good thing they didn't know what was in his mind.

He stopped by the galley and washed the blood from his face and hands with water from the barrel there,

then went on to Blackbeard's private cabin aft. There
he was alone, and he noted that, although it wasn't the
cleanest cabin he had ever seen, Blackbeard's own
private cabin was definitely in better shape than the
usual chaos on the deck outside. For some reason
Casca could not understand the pirate chief was playing a role. Not that the cabin was furnished in very
good taste. Any whore in London could have done a
better job.

With time on his hands, Casca prowled. On a
mahogany desk was an open ledger. Idly Casca turned
a few pages. Blackbeard's journal. One entry caught
Casca's eye:

"Such a day: rum all out; our company somewhat
sober; a damned confusion among us! Rogues
a-plotting; talk of separation. So I looked sharp for a
prize; such a day, took one with a great deal of liquor
on board, so kept the company hot, damned hot, then
all things went well again."

"Ah!"

Blackbeard was standing in the cabin door, a very
pleased look in his eyes. And behind him were Israel
Hands, the mates, and others not yet in Casca's view.

They all looked friendly—Blackbeard most of
all—and Casca was sure now that he was going to be
rewarded for his part in the fight.

He still disliked Blackbeard. He didn't have to have
any damn reason why, but now, with Blackbeard
standing momentarily in the hatchway, his face in part
shadow and light, Casca idly considered what there
was about the big bastard that turned him off.

The son of a bitch was hairy enough; Casca could not
recall offhand a man with such a black beard grown so
long. It came all the way up to his eyes, and he had

twisted it with ribbons in small tails after the manner of
the Ramillies wigs which were then in favor—and
which Casca thought had been designed by a group of
fruits. Anyhow, the way Blackbeard had these ribbons
turned about his ears suggested he was a fruit—
particularly since they were dark green.

But, shit! that wasn't enough to make Casca hate his
guts. Live and let live, he had always felt.

Blackbeard wore a scarlet sling over his shoulder
with three brace of pistols hanging in holsters like
bandoliers. No problem there. But the fur cap—a big,
thick, greasy fur cap in this weather! And Blackbeard
had stuck two lighted slow matches, one on each side,
under the cap—apparently trying to look like the per-
sonification of the Devil. Why would—.

"So, Master Cass Long, have you finished deciding
what I look like?"

The shadowed eyes were sharp and full of malice,
and Casca was surprised. His mind had just been getting ready to decide that Blackbeard wasn't bright
enough to lead a pirate nation, and McAdams was
betting on the wrong horse.

Blackbeard came into the cabin followed by the
others and pointed at the table that stood just in front of
the open rum locker.

"The head chair, if you please, Master Long. There
are a couple of matters. First, that of a reward." His
eyes gleamed in the light from the ship's lantern,
swinging in gimbals just over his head, and he was
probably smiling, though Casca could not really tell
because of the way the shadows fell on the black beard.

"Reward," Blackbeard repeated. "Damn my eyes,
but you're a good fighter."

He sat at the foot of the table and the others took

places on the sides. Two of the men—not officers, apparently just seamen—seemed a little uneasy. The others—the two mates and Israel Hands—had perfectly blank faces.

Something wasn't right here. Casca tensed.

"Now, this ship's council is officially in session. I declare it, and damn any man who says otherwise, says I. Agreed?"

One of the seaman started to open his mouth, but a glance from Israel Hands stopped him.

Ship's council? To reward a man? Casca didn't know much about pirates, but this didn't sound right to him.

"In the matter of Cass Long, passenger, en route to the command of Captain Tarleton Duncan, it is agreed that the said Cass Long hath rendered excellent service to my command and should be rewarded. Is this not so?"

"Aye." Only Israel Hands answered.

"In the commonwealth of pirates, he hath distinguished himself, and I hereby promote the said Cass Long to captain. May his soul be damned if he not be worthy. To captain, do you hear, Cass Long? But not of this vessel."

It was obvious that under that black beard the pirate chief was grinning widely, but there was still something in the eyes Casca could not place. Malice?

"Look sharp, men! Mates! Hands! Rum!"

There was a flurry of movement as they got up to do Blackbeard's bidding. As for the pirate chief, he kept his seat, his eyes on Casca.

Casca heard the clink of bottles in the cabinet behind him, then—

He heard absolutely nothing at all.

When Casca regained consciousness he was still in
the chair—but this time he was bound hand and foot,
tightly, with tarred ship's rope and gagged with his
own pistol sash. His sword was on the table—out of his
reach even if his hands had been unbound—and his
pistols were in the hands of Blackbeard who was toying
with them.

Again there was the strange light in Blackbeard's
eyes.

"Ah! Well, damnation, gentlemen. Our spy has
come to his senses." He reared back in his chair—like
a London solicitor, Casca thought—and surveyed the
men at the table with satisfaction. "Aye, that he hath.
Now, gentlemen—council members—are we agreed?"

"Aye." Again it was only Israel Hands who
answered.

Casca's head was beginning to throb with the pain
that had been masked while he was unconscious. Both
sides. Two of them must have got me at the same time,
he thought. Pistol butts? The way it was hurting it felt
more like belaying pins. He was trying to decide which
two had hit him. If he got out of this, he'd give the
bastards a taste of it.

Blackbeard's eyes steadied on Casca, and the light
in them was wicked. "You have been listening to the
proceedings of the council, have you not, Captain
Long? You have heard the testimony of Johnson and
Short here, have you not? That this new governor of the
Bahamas has planted a spy in our Brotherhood of the
Main, our Commonwealth of Pirates? That Johnson

saw you talking to a man we know is a lackey of the British government? Saw you in Montego Bay with this one? And Short himself overheard you admit you were such a spy? Look sharp, there, Short. You did hear such, did you not?''

"Aye.'' The little seaman looked like a rabbit cornered, but he spoke up pluckily enough.

"Aye. Now what do you say to that, Captain Long?'' Blackbeard leaned forward. "Look sharp, men. Let us hear what the good Captain Long has to say in his defense.'' He dropped the two pistols and made an exaggerated gesture of cupping his ear to hear better. "What do you hear, gentlemen? What does he say?''

The two seamen grinned, then thought better of it when they saw the impassive faces of the two mates and of Israel Hands.

"I don't hear anything. Do you, Captain Hands?''

"Nay, Captain.''

"Any of you other council members hear anything?''

Silence.

"Then let the record show that the spy, Captain Long, has nothing to say in his defense. As captain of this council I will pronounce sentence. One, says I, Captain Long, for being a spy, is to be hanged from the yardarm. Two, says I, sentence commuted to marooning, due to service rendered this command and due to the fact, well known by all in our Brotherhood, that in the commonwealth of pirates he who goes the greatest length of wickedness is a person of extraordinary gallantry and is therefore entitled to be distinguished by some high post, namely, promotion to captain in Master Long's case—and, damn my eyes, if spying is not wickedness, then, says I, what is? And, three, says I, until Captain Long is marooned—and upon his being marooned—said Captain Long shall remain bound, hand and foot, and shall have no food, no drink until such time as he is set ashore, and when he is set ashore, says I, he will still be bound and gagged, and no food, drink, supplies, or weapons shall be set ashore with him. And that, says I, just for the hell of it.''

Blackbeard grinned.

CHAPTER SEVEN

Two days later Casca lay in the bottom of the ship's boat being rowed to the island where he would be marooned. He was still bound hand and foot, and he was still gagged. He had no idea what island he was headed for. All he had been able to see from the deck when he was taken out and thrown into the boat before it was lowered was a quick glimpse of some island that had low hills and green trees.

"In the sunlight, damn it! Look sharp, men, and be quick about it."

That order had come from Blackbeard himself. The only officer aboard the longboat was the boatswain, a silent man made even quieter by the fact that at the moment he was too drunk to do anything but stare stupidly dead ahead. Casca was lying at his feet, so the boatswain's drunk face was all he could see. Unlike most of the pirates, the boatswain was gaunt—hungry looking. He paid no attention at all to Casca.

The oars slapped against the water, and Casca could feel the vibration of the boat's passage through the relatively mild surf. None of the pirates said anything. Some inner intuition told Casca they were apprehensive—but that didn't make sense. Why fear an island?

As for Casca, his already strong hatred of Blackbeard was beginning to be reinforced by a definite desire to rip the blustering bastard's face off him. Casca had the feeling that the way he was being set up was just too damn smooth. It was as if the bearded bastard back there on the ship was making fun of him. Like the way a cat plays around with a mouse—playing with it as though it wasn't worth anything. The drumhead court-martial was one thing, but Casca might have been able to go along with that just because Blackbeard was a stupid bastard jealous to the extreme. But with the island showing up in less than two hours . . . Shit! Blackbeard had it all planned in advance. Whether it had something to do with Tarleton Duncan that Casca didn't know about, or whether it was just the way Blackbeard's twisted mind worked he didn't know. But it made no difference. Somehow, he was going to even the score.

Only trouble was, at the moment he wasn't in much of a position to do anything about it.

The boat beached, and the pirates pulled it up just enough on the smooth sand to keep it from going back into the sea. In silence—which by now had begun to bother Casca—they pulled him from the longboat and dragged him up the beach, not too far out of reach of the water, and propped him up against a rock in the sun. The rock was hot against his back. He was facing seaward. He could see the pirate ship lying off the shoal water, and he thought he could make out the figure of Blackbeard holding a spyglass on him.

"Let's get the hell out of here."

The pirate who said it had a worried tone to his voice, and Casca could see that he didn't want to stay there a moment longer. It was the first words spoken by any of the pirates, and now they all hurried back to the longboat, pushed it into the water, jumped aboard, and began rowing quickly back toward the ship. They had, in fact, been in such a rush that when they dumped him on the sand one of the pirates had accidentally and unknowingly dropped a piece of eight he had apparently been carrying in one of his pistol holsters, and the coin had gone down into the folds of the cravat around Casca's neck.

Now why are they in such a rush? Shit! I've got myself involved with madmen, he thought. Already the sun was beginning to make him uncomfortable. What Blackbeard had in mind, of course, was to have him broiled alive out here. However . . .

They had tied him up with tarred ship's rope. The heat of the sun would soften the tar—plus the pirates who had tied him, either by accident or design, had left some slight slack. He watched the longboat reach the ship and be taken aboard. The sails were unfurled. They caught the brief wind, and *The Queen's Revenge* stood out to sea. By the time she would be hull down on the horizon and beyond spyglass range he could have himself untied. No big damage done—except for postponing his voyage to America a bit longer.

He began flexing his wrists and felt the rope give slightly. There was still the problem of how to get off this damn island—but, first things first.

He worried slightly because of the pirate crew's

apparent fear of the island. But only for a moment.
After all, what could happen to him on a deserted
island?

What he didn't know was that the island wasn't
deserted . . . .

Six pairs of very dark eyes were watching Casca.
The eyes of six men. Spaniards.

The island on which Blackbeard had marooned
Casca happened to be one tiny spot of land in a wide
area of the Caribbean. Actually it was the top of an
extinct volcano—but none of the men on it knew that.
Not even Casca.

It was not on the British Admiralty charts. Nor any
other charts. But it was known by quite a few pirate
captains, Spanish as well as those of Blackbeard's
Brotherhood.

And, over a period of time, Spanish pirate captains
had marooned malefactors. Several dozen, as a matter
of fact, but not more than a baker's dozen had survived.

Brotherhood captains had also marooned men on the
island. And, since they were enemies afloat, they remained enemies ashore. So, when Casca was put
ashore there were thirteen Spanish maroons and fifteen
Brotherhood maroons, organized loosely into two
groups fighting each other. Since they had neither guns
nor swords they had to fight with rocks and sticks.
They also made crude bows from tropical trees that
were really too soft for the purpose and wooden spears,
points hopefully hardened in campfire flames. The
lack of good weapons made killing each other off
rather difficult, but, given enough time, both sides had

managed. It was helpful to discover—as in Casca's case—a new maroon of the other side since it was much easier to kill him. The six Spaniards in the cover of the vegetation at the forest's edge were not in for a bit of fun. The Brotherhood maroons, they knew, were encamped on the other side of the island, held there by ineffective—but intimidating—archery fire from the other seven Spaniards. These six would have the pleasure of killing Casca. Since life on the island was boring—there was enough fruit to eat, but nothing else to do—killing was a nice break from the everyday routine.

The Spanish leader—by temporary sufferance only; there was no discipline among the maroons—checked the horizon to be sure the ship was not coming back, and then signaled his men. They came out into the open, but then stopped when the leader held up his hand, then pointed at Casca.

That one, unaware that he had company, was busily engaged in wriggling out of his ropes. He was making progress but it was going slow. Watching him provided some amusement for the Spaniards. They were going to kill him anyway. Might as well enjoy watching him struggle. So all six hunkered down on the sand and, grinning, waited for him to either succeed or give up.

It took him the better part of a quarter hour, but he succeeded. Finally free, he stood up, rubbed his wrists, stamped his feet to bring the circulation back, and removed the gag. Then he turned around.

And, as he turned, the six Spaniards rose to their feet, clubs poised.

Casca stared at them.

"Bastard son of an English dog," the Spanish leader

greeted him in Spanish. *"Bastardo. Desecho. Lechón."* The Spaniard was not very imaginative, and his remarks on Casca's lineage were far from original. Casca had heard much better from amateur English whores. He smiled—and that infuriated all six Spaniards who began shouting obscenities at him, clubs raised.

Casca laughed.

After Blackbeard and his twisted thinking it was such a pleasure to see normal men—even if they were ready to kill him—that Casca felt a warm glow of pleasure.

"By the blood of the Virgin, Herself!" he exclaimed in Spanish. "You bastards are the best things I've seen in days."

"Que? You speak Spanish, Englishman?" The Spanish leader looked confused.

Spanish? Hell, it was only bastard Latin. Casca did not explain, but he did grin.

The Spanish maroons hesitated and got into an argument amongst themselves. The net result, though, was that since he had come from Blackbeard's ship he must be an enemy.

It took a little while, but Casca convinced the Spaniards that he would make a better recruit than a target. That settled, there was one other problem.

"You help us fight the English. Now we beat hell out of them bastards." The Spanish leader grinned.

"English? What English?" Casca asked.

"On the other side of the island."

"You mean you aren't the only ones on this island?"

"Pero, no, mi amigo." The Spaniard proceeded to

explain to Casca about the marooned Brotherhood pirates and about the continuing war between the two groups. Casca looked at him and at the other five. They were all in rags, and they were all skinny. Casca didn't know too much about these little islands, but he guessed there was probably fruit to eat and not much else. Even if there were—wild goats or such—these maroons were too busy fighting each other to hunt.

"How many?"

"*Que?*"

"You. Spaniards. And the others."

"Ah . . ." The Spaniard started counting on his fingers.

But another one of the pirates, a young fellow with a very skimpy beard, said: "Twenty-eight. You make twenty-nine."

Twenty-nine men. Casca thought about that, his eyes watching the far horizon of the blue ocean.

"What you see?" the Spaniard sounded suspicious.

"How to get off this island," Casca growled.

Twenty-nine men. That meant two things. One, a lot of pirate ships must stop here to maroon that many men, Brotherhood or Spanish. Two, twenty-nine men were a large enough crew to sail a captured ship. . . .

He turned back to the Spaniards and explained what he had in mind.

"No! It would not work! We will not make peace with the English dogs!"

"Suit yourself," Casca shrugged. "But I'm getting off."

"No!" The clubs came up.

"Oh, shit!" Casca grumbled, and made one quick movement forward and to the side. It was something he had learned long ago, taught by that old friend from the land of Chin. The next thing the Spanish leader knew there was a swift kick in his gut, low down, very low down, that temporarily interrupted his interest in the proceedings. There were other movements, too. A blow to the side of the throat of the oldest bearded Spaniard. A twisting motion here. Another there.

They had the clubs, but Casca had the ability. Hell, not one of them could have lasted five minutes in a Roman arena. In half that time Casca had four Spaniards out and a fifth backing away. Only the young Spaniard with the skimpy beard still faced him, still holding a club, but not moving—not scared, but with an appraising look in his young eyes.

Casca had not bothered to pick up any of the clubs that now lay on the rocky ground on the border between underbrush and beach. He, too, had an appraising look in his eyes, studying the young Spaniard.

"See what I mean?" Casca said in Spanish, not moving on the youngster.

"*Sí.*"

Casca looked down at the leader.

"Have we got a deal?"

"Ah . . ."

"Look, dammit, I could have ripped your face off and smashed what little brains you have if I had wanted to. And that goes for the rest of you bastards. I didn't, you sons of bitches, because we need each other if we're going to take the next damn ship that puts in here."

"But we have no swords, no guns. . . ."

"So? With twenty-nine men I can take any ship's boat that puts in here."

Which really wasn't exactly true, but it sounded like it to them if not to Casca.

Casca's Spaniards—he was beginning to think of them as his own private squad—took him over the mountain to the other side of the island. It was a night's long march under a bright full moon, and the Spaniards apparently had no fear of being ambushed by the discarded members of the Brotherhood.

"The fort," the young Spaniard explained when Casca asked him.

"Fort?"

"*Sí.*"

They were walking a well-worn path under the trees surprisingly open for the tropics, and the silver moonlight dappled the way. Casca reflected upon other hills he had walked as a young boy, younger then than his erstwhile guide was now. But he liked the young man very much. There was a clean quality to him that was not found often in the world. He wondered what crime had brought him to this sorry state. Of course there were times when the innocent passengers of ships taken by the pirates were not killed but left abandoned on deserted isles. This might have been the case with his young guide.

Julio, the young Catalonian, explained about the fort and gave Casca a rundown on the relations between the English and the Spaniards. It was what was to be expected. They didn't get along worth a shit.

As for the fort, none knew who had originally built it or why. They would have liked to have known because whoever it was had to have had an axe—or at the very least some kind of adz to cut and shape the logs. Such a weapon in their hands now could mean control of the island. At any rate some long dead castaways had built a small fort of logs over a spring on the east side of the island. Whoever controlled the fort, with its continuous water supply, had the edge when the time of no rains came, which occurred with great frequency. As it was, the fort was now in the hands of the maroons left here by the Brotherhood.

Dawn had just reddened the eastern sky when Casca and his group reached the fort. They hid themselves about a hundred yards from it. The fort itself was not a very prepossessing affair. Actually it looked more like a shack of weathered logs.

Casca stepped out into the open. He was holding a white rag—torn from his own cravat—tied to a stick as a flag of truce.

He was met by a barrage of stones thrown from the fort. Fortunately, the aim was not too good.

"Knock that shit off!" he yelled, and kept going closer.

The English words got him in. Inside proved to be little more than a stockade since there was no roof. The Brotherhood maroons were carbon copies of the Spanish—except that they had a leader, a real leader, a big, dour, one-armed Scot who must have been several inches over six feet tall.

Casca had to look up to him, and that didn't do his disposition any good. "Don't you know what a flag of truce is?" he demanded.

"Aye."

"Then, why—"

Casca did not get to finish the sentence. He had gotten too damn confident. Whatever it was that now hit him on the back of the neck took care of that.

The last thing he saw was the smile on the face of the one-armed giant.

CHAPTER EIGHT

When Casca came to, he found he had been tied up with vines and thrown against the wall of the fort. He looked down at the vines holding his feet. They didn't seem too tough. He ought to be out of them in no time. His hands were tied behind him. He tried stretching his arms to pull the lashing apart.

Damn! The vines were tougher than they looked. No luck at all. Behind him he could feel an opening in the wall, a wide space between the logs, and he tried to feel if there was a sharp edge he might cut the vines with. No. The logs were smooth as polished marble.

The Brotherhood castaways had not bothered to gag him. As a matter of fact they seemed to have forgotten him entirely—tied him up, thrown him against the wall, and left him alone. That was a hell of a note. Casca had been in tight spots before—plenty of them—but he couldn't remember when he had been completely ignored.

He looked at the pirates, trying to decide which ones might have hit him, but there was really no way of telling. Oh, hell, he would just give it to all of them.

The big one-armed Scotsman was gone. So were half a dozen of the others—the ones who had been there when he came in with his flag of truce. The fort had been relatively crowded then with all fifteen men. Now he counted only eight. Had they made some kind of deal with the Spaniards? But just when he had the thought there came a shouted curse—in Spanish—from somewhere outside the walls, followed by a small shower of stones. The Brotherhood men paid no attention. They were hunkered down in a rough semicircle, and Casca saw one of them pound a large object on a stone. Coconuts! It must be breakfast time.

But where had the others gone? And how had they gotten past the Spaniards outside?

He looked around the fort. Actually it was simply an area enclosed by crudely stacked trees with the smaller limbs broken off where possible and the open spaces filled in with brush and stones—evidence that the men who built it had no tools, no axe, hatchet, or saw. In fact, Casca could see that the ends of the logs were burned. So that was the way the men who had built the structure had downed the trees: built a fire around the base and burned them down. To Casca it seemed like an awful lot of unnecessary trouble. But if the predecessors of these men had the patience to go through all that trouble, maybe he could get these to storm the first ship that landed.

But he had to get loose first.

He still had not figured out how the others had left. But suddenly old memories came back into his brain, memories of the lands where he had first served, memories of shepherd camps he had seen in the past . . .

There ought to be—

Ah! There was.

The spring was not in the center of the stockade, but over to one side, and there were a couple of rough lean-tos against the stockade walls. The spring came out of rock, out of a kind of hillock that rose up there, and the wall on that side was built up over a spur of rock laid down by some long-dead volcano—and Casca had known about volcanic rock since his childhood. He didn't really expect to find a cave here on this Caribbean island, but—

Hell! It wasn't much of a cave, just a small tunnel in the rock only a little larger than it took for a man to wriggle into. And it was partially hidden by trash, branches and rocks the pirates had pulled over it. But the ground showed that the brush had been moved repeatedly. And if this was like the ones Casca had known elsewhere the passageway would get wider inside. A "blowhole" would have formed in the molten lava when the volcano had last erupted—a long, long time ago. And somewhere out in the forest, up on the side of the hill, probably now hidden by trees, there would be an opening where the earth had fallen through. An easy way out. Now, why hadn't the Spaniards known about that? It bothered Casca. He had been counting on the Spaniards to be smart. But, then, he hadn't been too smart himself, getting taken by the big one-armed Scot—

"Captain Long . . ."

The voice behind Casca, outside the wall, was so soft he barely heard it. But the words were in Spanish. *Julio!*

All Casca could do was rub his bound wrists against the log behind him.

"Silencio, señor." This time the whisper was little more than a breath.

Casca could feel the fingers of the young Spanish boy probing gently into the open space between the logs, touching his wrists and exploring the knotted vine. Casca considered the logs he could see opposite him. They were crudely stacked, yes, and there was space between them, but he doubted that the boy would have room enough to untie the vines. The probing stopped.

"Un momento." This time the whisper was louder, and Casca worried that the youngster would get too loud, loud enough for the pirates to hear. Besides that, how had the boy, in broad daylight, gotten to the wall in the first place? And how had he known where to find Casca?

Casca began to sweat.

Then he felt the fingers back in the log opening, and something cold and hard touched his bound wrists. A knife? Did any of these men have knives? The glint of metal he thought he had seen on the one-armed man's chest, was it a hidden knife?

There was a sawing motion on the vines holding his wrists. Evidently Julio was trying to cut him loose. At that moment one of the pirates in the group opposite looked straight at Casca, and Casca felt instinctively that the man knew something was going on. He tried to return the pirate's gaze with a noncommittal look of his own, and he saw that the pirate was holding a broken shard of the black volcanic rock, the stuff that looked like glass, obsidian. As Casca watched, the pirate used the rock flake like a knife to cut off a slice of the white coconut meat and stuff it into his mouth.

So that was what Julio had, a sharp rock. It would

take a long time to cut through the vines. No, that wasn't right. The glass rock was sharper than steel. Casca had seen men shave with it. His wrists would be free shortly. But there would still be the problem of the vines around his ankles. Well, he would worry about that when the time came. In the meantime, if there was obsidian on the island, why hadn't the men used it to make better weapons? The only explanation Casca could think of was the the pirates who were marooned were not necessarily the smartest men in the world. But that didn't hold water either. What about young Julio? He seemed like a pretty sharp kid.

Shit! Casca complained to himself. Here I go thinking again. And every time I do it I get my ass in a sling. Thinking about his ass reminded him that he needed to piss—but that didn't seem to be something that he was going to be able to do in the immediate future. He glanced furtively at the ground around him to see if there was a sharp rock on which he might try cutting his ankles loose. No luck. There were a couple of clubs lying on the soft earth within easy reach of his hands, but nothing useful for freeing his feet. Damn! He couldn't go for the clubs until his feet were free.

At the moment he came to that conclusion, he felt the vines loosen from around his wrists. His hands were now free, but that was all Julio could do for him. Almost all—he felt the sharp rock, warmed by Julio's hand and the friction of sawing the vines, being pushed into his opened palm. Well, he had a weapon—of sorts—but there was damn little he could do with it.

At that moment, the brush hiding the tunnel entrance moved aside and the one-armed Scot wriggled out into the stockade, followed by four of his men.

● ● ●

Outside the palisade wall, Julio, having freed Casca's wrists, now found himself in a tough situation. He had gotten to the fort in the first place by crawling through the grass that lay in the deep shadow cast by the early morning sun and the stockade wall. He had found Casca by his scent—the scar-faced stranger was so soon from a ship that he still smelled of things not on the island: rum and tobacco and the other elusive but well-remembered odors of life aboard ship, as well as the tarred ropes that had bound him. It wasn't hard to find him outside the wall, and Julio felt proud of himself for using his nose. He also felt proud for having brought the sharp stone along and for having cut Casca's wrists loose.

But now he was trapped. The sun had climbed up in the sky. There were no more shadows to hide in, not so long as the noon approached.

He huddled against the wall, knowing he had a long, long time to wait.

"Who the hell are you?"

The one-armed Scot had come over to Casca and now hunkered down in front of him—but well out of reach. The Scot had black, feisty eyes under heavy eyebrows. He carried an air of constant suspicion. Casca considered him. The big man looked like a troublemaker all right, and it wasn't hard to figure out how he must have gotten himself marooned.

"I asked you a question, you bastard. Who are you?"

Now that was something Casca would have to think about. Again he did not answer right off but continued staring into the Scot's eyes until something happened.

He could see mirrored in the feisty black eyes something of what the Scot saw in him, and instantly he knew that the Scot had seen the iced water coldness of death in his own gray-blue eyes. He had looked deep into the utter ruthlessness that could be Casca, and had the shit scared out of him, even though Casca was bound and apparently helpless—but the Scot did not show his fear. Casca knew he had him, so he answered him:

"Captain Cass Long, late a passenger aboard *The Queen's Revenge*, Captain Teach commanding, Israel Hands, master. En route to the command of Captain Tarleton Duncan." He rolled the words out of his mouth in the stately manner that was now the fashion, all the while his eyes fixed sharply on the Scot.

The big man scowled, looked back over his shoulder, and called, "McLean!"

A scrawny little fellow with darting, rat eyes detached himself from the group and scurried over to the Scot.

"You're the latest one to come aboard, excepting, of course, this one with the scar on his face. D'ye recall kenning a mon name o' Captain Teach?"

McLean's rat eyes grew wide, and his small mouth smirked. "Aye. 'Tis the devil himself. Blackbeard."

"Blackbeard?"

"Aye."

"Ah!"

"Look," Casca interrupted, "let's cut this shit. I want to get off this godforsaken island"—he deliberately made his voice rise in volume—"and I know damn well your men want to get off it too."

"Laddie, y're in naw position t' get off nawt."

"Like hell. I know how to do it, and you've been sitting on your butt."

The Scot started to hit him, then thought better of it. "Talk," he growled.

"All right. What I say you do is stop this damned fighting shit between you and the Spaniards. Get together. Organize. Lay for the next ship that puts in here—from the look of how many of you there are on this asshole of an island there must be more damn ships sailing here than there are tits in a Bristol whorehouse—take her, and get back to the sea where the plunder is. Ain't a goddamn man among you's going to get rich squatting on his duff on this hunk of sand eating coconuts."

Casca had been loud enough. The men had come up. Now they were in a semicircle ranged around the big Scot, grinning.

One big-fisted, red-haired, ruddy-faced fellow even said: "Fucking good thinking, mate."

The big Scot raised his one arm and scratched his nose with his thumb. "And how d'ye plan to take a ship, seeing as how we've nawt to fight wi'? Nae sword, nae gun, nae weapon o' any kind, me bucko."

"There are fifteen of you. There are thirteen Spaniards. More than enough men to take on the crew of a ship—particularly if you lure one of them away and take his weapons."

"Lure? It's going to be luring, aye? And how d'ye think y're aboot t' lure a mon wi' a wee gun or so?"

Casca told him—and the men roared with laughter.

But the Scot was dubious.

"It'll nae work. There's not a mon here—"

"You forget the Spanish."

"But we fight the Spanish."

"Damn your fighting. You want to get your ass off this damn island, don't you?"

The Scot hesitated.

That was when a distant voice came from somewhere high up on the mountain behind them.

"Halloo the fort! Halloo! Sail ho! Sail ho! East-south-east-by east. Sail ho! Sail ho!"

"Now!" Casca shouted. "Now's the opportunity. What about it?"

But the Scot still hesitated.

Oh, shit! Casca thought. He didn't have the time to argue. He brought his hands around, pushed himself unsteadily erect on his bound feet, picked up a club, and smashed the Scot in his thick skull before the dumbfounded pirates—shocked motionless by his apparently magical eruption—could react.

"Dammit!" he said. "There's no time to waste! Call the Spaniards! Look lively, you bastards! It's now or never!"

He bent over, and with his left hand began sawing at the vines on his ankles, using the stone Julio had given him—and keeping a weather eye out for the crew.

For half a dozen heartbeats it all hung in the balance. Then the red-haired Englishman bellowed:

"You heard the captain! Hop to it, mates! Lively, now! Lively!"

Casca was free. He called to the Spaniards. There was an answering halloo in Spanish.

Now if these morons would only work together for a little while . . .

Human beings are the damndest animals, Casca thought, looking at the pirates grouped before him out on the open slope of the hill a couple of hundred yards from the fort but out of sight of it. Spanish and English. An hour ago they had been at each other's throats. Now here they were, standing together.

Well, not exactly together. The Spaniards were more or less on one side, the English on the other. But they were more interested in what he had to say than in braining each other.

"Pero, thees 'lure," Senor Capitan Loong"— Garcia, the fat Spaniard (the only fat man on the island), was trying manfully to speak in English— "who thees one she esta?"

Casca told him.

And Julio—who had not hitherto been consulted on the matter—yelled, "By the Mother of God, no! I will not! No! No! But never!"

"You want to stay on this shitass island?"

"But—Honor!—" Julio went off into Spanish so fervent and rapid that even Casca could not keep up with it.

And that was when the lookout up on the mountain yelled, "Sail making for the island!"

Casca called: "What kind of ship?"

"Sloop."

"There! That does it! A sloop we can take." He turned to Julio and said in Spanish, "This is one we can handle. What about it?"

The young Spaniard looked despairingly around at the semicircle of pirates. One of the Brotherhood men spat—to leeward—and said: "Shit, kid, ain't nobody going to hold it against you." The words meant nothing to Julio, but he understood the tone.

"All right. Now—"

"Captain!" One of the quieter Brotherhood men, a Yorkshireman by the look of him, interrupted. "I can improve on what you had in mind."

"How?"

"I spend four years apprenticed to a portrait painter in London." The pirate's voice was soft and his diction unexpectedly above the servant class. Casca guessed he probably preferred boys to girls, but that was his business. Now his deep blue eyes were looking questioningly at Casca. "I want to get off this island, too," he added.

"What do you have in mind?" There wasn't much time. If the sloop was making any headway at all—and judging by the stiff breeze coming in from the sea she ought to be—they had less than an hour to set up an ambush.

"If the captain please, leave that to me."

Hell! Why not? There were other matters he had to tend to. "All right. But step lively, dammit!" He looked out to sea where the top of the sloop's mast was now becoming visible from the beach. He would have to get his men in position—he had never seen the terrain farther down the beach where the sloop would land—if it landed

If it passed by—now that, dammit, would tear it all. But he didn't mention his fear to the men. He headed them down toward the landing and then momentarily looked back out to sea. More of the sail was now visible. The sloop was making good time.

Casca wondered what the sloop's captain was doing at the moment. He certainly wouldn't be expecting twenty-nine men to ambush his men and take over his ship.

CHAPTER NINE

The sloop's captain was standing aft by the rail, holding a half-empty bottle of rum by the neck, idly watching the black slaves work his ship, and thinking of nothing in particular. The one female slave, naked from the navel up, was leaning against the rail to the leeward side watching the green shape of the island come up out of the water. The female slave was the captain's personal property, but at the moment he was not looking at her, nor was anyone else. The way she was standing the big teats on her full brown breasts pointed down at the whispering green sea and swayed with the roll of the ship. Leaning against the rail she had a little the look of a cow—but of a cow that had been milked too often.

"Put yet into idt der Godt-damn butts!" the captain suddenly roared at the slaves forward. His mulatto third mate obediently brandished his whip.

Slaves! The captain was in a foul mood, and he was more than willing to take it out on the slaves. He was running a cargo of sugar. The hold was packed with hogsheads, and there were even half a dozen or so lashed on deck. The sugar hogsheads were heavy, overloading the sloop, making her ride very low in the water, and the extra tonnage would probably have slowed her down had she not already been hampered by the heavy barnacle growth on her old hull. The captain was a mean, brutal, small-minded lout—but he was also a reasonably competent seaman. If this ancient sloop were not careened and the barnacles scraped from her she would take forever to make the passage to New Orleans—if she made it at all. He had sailed these waters a long time. He could practically smell the storms that were coming. And overloaded as the sloop was she would founder. What he really needed to do was throw some of the sugar overboard. But the greed that had put the sugar on in the first place was the greed that would keep it aboard.

This island, now. Not on the charts—but that didn't necessarily mean anything. What he could count on was that she was most certainly uninhabited—otherwise she would be on a chart. And if there was a flat beach at all, then he could careen his vessel and get the barnacles off. At least that was what had gone through his mind, but there had been something else, too. If he was right in sensing that a storm was brewing, it would probably come about the time they finished the careening, and he could take shelter somewhere about the island—if there was a suitable anchorage. None of this did he discuss with his first mate, the only other white man aboard, an old man, maybe over fifty, whose chief pleasure in life seemed to be seeing the blood run from the whip marks on a black slave's back. Vell, to every man his pleasure. . . .

He glanced casually at the black female slave, and the left corner of his mouth lifted beneath the shaggy mustache. She was the only woman aboard, and she was strictly for his use only. He could imagine how that galled the other officers—and maybe even the slaves, too, though they, of course, were mere cattle. Seeing those big brown tits and not being able to do anything about it . . .

Ah!

Momentarily the captain was almost happy. He swung the rum bottle to his lips and took a long pull. . . .

They made the island at about the middle of the day, and, yes, there was an anchorage. More, there was a long stretch of gently sloping white beach backed by a stand of big coconut palms whose trunks were sturdy enough to take tackle. Soundings with the lead—as well as the color of the water—showed a drop-off and a gradient ideal for careening. All that momentarily bothered the captain. The site was too perfect. He swept his spyglass carefully over the entire area, looking for signs that other ships before him had careened here, but there was only the virgin land. So! Vas not only yet der uncharted island, vas one nodt yet found. Immediately he ordered the beginning of the careening, now in the hot middle of the day, seeing with pleasure the dark looks he got not only from the slave crew but from his own officers. Any reasonable captain would have waited until the cool of the evening. Ah! The boat he now sent ashore he put in the charge of the first mate, knowing that that individual hated the boatswain's guts, and the two of them would not be likely to get together against him. Besides, the first mate had an odd passion for weapons. If he behaved as he usually did, he would be wearing a double brace of pistols, a long dirk, cutlass, and carrying a musket double-loaded. Not the kind of man to let a slave get away.

Ja!

Damn all slaves! Carter Jenkins, first mate of the sloop *Odysseus*, lounged in the stern sheets of the ship's boat, pulled up on the white sand of the beach, and waited while the wiry little mulatto boatswain organized his slave crew. There was the matter of the big hawser to be carried to the line of coconut palms—and sundry other matters. Jenkins paid very little attention to that. Though he thoroughly despised the little boatswain he was satisfied that the mulatto knew his job. As a matter of fact he envied the little bastard his competence; that was one of the reasons for his hatred. The boatswain would take care of things nicely. Oh, after everything was set up he, Jenkins, might be able to find some little something to bitch about and make life a little unpleasant for the boatswain—but let that come later. Right now Jenkins had other things on his mind.

What he mostly had on his mind was the women he was going to have when they got to New Orleans. Silently he cursed the captain for dangling that female slave in front of them all the time—particularly the bit about taking her out on deck and having her bathe under the ship's pump. He knew exactly why the captain did it—and the son of a bitch had succeeded. Well . . . He would have been horny enough anyway.

Jenkins was past fifty and that made a difference in the execution—but not in the anticipation. As a matter of fact, he admitted to himself, maybe there was more anticipation now than when he was young. After a long voyage he dreamed of women, thought of women, even imagined sometimes that he saw their phantom images, like the mirages on the desert that time the Tripoli pirates had held him captive.

So now, in the noonday tropical sun, only partially protected by the wide-brimmed hat he wore—the sun no reasonable white man would ever go out in—he half expected to see the images of naked women in the dancing air over the hot beach.

He didn't, though, so his attention came back to the second pleasure in his life, the possibility of killing one of these dmaned slaves. They were like children. Now that they were ashore they were probably dreaming of making a dash for the underbrush. Which was really the reason Jenkins was still sitting out here in the stern of the longboat broiling his brains in the sun. He wanted them to think they had a chance. Then he would get the first one who tried to run away. In Jenkins' experience, there was always at least one who tried it. He looked forward to shooting slaves—or anything else for that matter. Jenkins did not particularly like using a blade. He was pretty good with a cutlass if he had to be, but he never liked it. Truth was, he wanted to stay just a little distance away from whatever he killed, and a blade meant too close contact.

Now a woman, though . . . Close contact was fine there. Yeah . . . Real fine . . .

Jenkins sighed and stood up—unsteadily—in the longboat. It was pulled up far enough on the beach not to be washed out, but it still swayed a little as he stood upright. Hell! he thought. I got too much going through my mind. His nerves were on edge and he suddenly felt like something was going to happen—but he didn't know what. But he thought it was going to be something good, something to look forward to. That was the trouble about getting old. There wasn't all that much to look forward to. Jenkins spat into the water and got out of the longboat.

He had spotted a smooth rock in the shade of a tree and headed for it. The rock would make a good place to sit and watch that little bastard mulatto boatswain struggle with his slaves to get the hawsers around the trees and the tackle set up. It was a nice flat rock with an open space behind it and underbrush coming up on both sides. In a way it was kinda like a stage. After he got his fill of women in New Orleans, maybe he'd go to a theater, watch a play. Wouldn't be as much fun as bedding a whore, but it would be something to do. Now if only—

Damn!

He had seen one!

An image of a woman!

Right behind the rock on which he was going to sit.

Just for a moment, but real as you please. And damned if she wasn't a white woman! Naked from the waist up. Big boobs. Damn! but they were big! And round! Biggest, whitest boobs he had seen on a woman—real, dream, or fantasy—in years. Young face—or at least that was the way he remembered it. Even had a big flower in her hair.

By damn, if these were the kind of daydreams he was going to have on this island, why, hell, this was going to be a nice time. Jenkins made for the rock.

When he sat on it, it occurred to him he'd better take another look at the slaves. But they were hard at work, and he saw that, even if the image he had seen had been no more than his own private fantasy none of the slaves nor the boatswain could have seen it because of the underbrush beside the rock. That was the trouble with a daydream that vivid. Seemed so real you always felt somebody else could see it—

What the hell?

Jenkins would have sworn he could smell the flower that had been in the woman's hair.

There it was agin. Strong. Must be flowers behind him. He turned his head to look.

But there was only green underbrush, and, in the opening, a path leading back up the hillside. A path that must have been there for some time because it was loose sand, and—

In that loose sand, clear as the nose on a man's face, was the imprint of a bare foot.

Damn! Jenkins decided he had better lay off that cheap rum that they had put aboard when they took on the cargo. Not only was he dreaming of seeing naked-titted women where there were no women, now he was seeing her footprint. For a fraction of a second he started to reach out and touch the footprint in the sand to see if it were real or not, but he jerked back his hand before it was halfway there. He just didn't want any hard evidence interfering with the truth he already knew existed: that both the image of the woman and the footprint were mere figments of his imagination.

Unfortunately he did look back up the hill into the shadows under the trees—

And saw the naked woman again passing quickly across his view, big boobs and all.

That was just a little too much. Jenkins glanced at the slaves, called to the boatswain: "Watch them. I'm going to look for a spring up here"—and started up the path.

Almost immediately it made a sharp turn to the right,

and again he smelled the strong perfumed odor of the flowers. When the path turned back again it was in a relatively dark, narrow space between another high rock and the close-growing underbrush, and there was something white on the path. Involuntarily Jenkins looked down at the patch of white. He had not quite finished identifying it for what it was—a pile of flower blossoms—when Casca's club hit the back of his head. . . .

The boatswain was not fond of the first mate, Jenkins, though he did not share the older man's hatred. To the boatswain hatred was a luxury a stupid man could not afford, and the boatswain knew he was not the smartest fellow afloat. What he did he did well, but that was because he had worked at it a long time and because there was always somebody over him that he could go to if it looked like there might be a problem. The boatswain had no intention of being left by himself.

The first ten minutes Jenkins was gone "looking for a spring" were no problem for the boatswain. The next five were. And the five after that threw him into a panic. Being in sole control of the gang setting up the hawsers didn't bother him. He'd done it many times. But being in sole control of the landing party with the first mate unaccountably missing was something else. He kept looking over at the rock, expecting the mate to appear. When the mate didn't, and the boatswain knew he had to do something about it, he had a problem with what to do with the slaves. His solution was not all that bright. He ordered all of them to stand in a group out on the open beach, but not too close to the boat. He edged over the rock, trying to keep his eyes on the men,

holding both pistols aimed at them, and at the same
time trying to grab quick glances back into the forest.

Naturally this whole activity was of substantial interest to the slaves who had not heretofore thought their
boatswain mad.

It was of considerably more interest to the captain
who had chosen that particular moment to turn his
brass spyglass onto the island to see if the boatswain
and first mate were making as much progress there as
his second and third mates were with shifting the big
hogsheads of sugar out of the hold and onto one side of
the deck.

What the hell!

The captain was momentarily speechless. What he
saw in the spyglass was the band of slaves grouped
together on the open beach. Neither the boatswain nor
the first mate were in evidence since the angle at which
the shoreline cut in hid the rock where the first mate
had disappeared from the captain's view.

The captain called the second mate to his side and
thrust the spyglass into his grasp. ''Look! Und, vill you
tell me v'at d' dom hell you see?''

Meanwhile, the boatswain was having his problems.
Trying to keep his eyes on his slaves, look up the hill,
and get over the rock was all just a little too much for
him. So, where the underbrush was thinner he backed
into it so that he could still see his men.

Once in the underbrush and beside the rock he
found, like the mate, that he had to make a turn, and
that took him out of sight of the slaves altogether
causing him to panic completely. He had a very good
idea of what the captain would do to him if he let the
slaves escape. So he did two things at once: he tried to

turn around and get back out—and in the process tangled the cutlass hanging from his hip in the underbrush—and he opened his mouth to yell for the first mate, cursing himself inwardly for not thinking of doing that in the first place.

Unfortunately for him, at the moment when he was trying to turn around, his eyes swept over the opening farther up the path and he saw the woman—flower in hair, naked boobs, skirt just below the navel.

Up to this point it had not been a good day for the boatswain. Now it was totally shot. The yell for the mate stopped at his tonsils. His mouth dropped open and reflex made both his hands come up, pointing his two pistols at the spot where the woman had just been.

Whether the boatswain saw anything else would be impossible to ascertain. He hadn't gotten far enough into the underbrush to get what had been planned for him, so the nearest pirate stood up and threw his club. It was a fairly heavy club, and it was thrown with considerable force, and it was followed by a club thrown from the other side by a second pirate who was afraid the first pirate had screwed everything up. As a consequence the first club hit him sideways, full on the side of the neck, breaking that relatively frail part of his body—and the second, coming a little later, got him as he was falling, the heavy part of the club hitting the thin part of his skull over his temple.

It was all pretty noisy, so noisy that the slaves on the beach heard some of it—the strangled cry from the boatswain's throat, the clatter of his cutlass hanger hitting the rock, the fall of the pistols, the very loud thwack! of the two clubs coming together when they finished him off, and the thrashing of his dying body in the underbrush. These were not sounds to inspire confidence, and the general feeling was that they should take to their heels at what might be a supernatural event.

Well, take to their heels they did—but toward the forest and freedom, not away from it.

The view from the sloop, though, was confusing. The second mate had the spyglass to his eye at the time, and what he saw was the slaves suddenly break and run as a body toward the forest. Since the ship was too far away for him to hear the noise of the boatswain's demise and since he couldn't see the boatswain, it merely looked to him and to the captain—who could see the group itself without the spyglass—as though the slaves were responding to some odd command of the first mate or the boatswain.

That damn first mate, was the captain's unspoken conclusion. American. All Americans were crazy.

So the work of moving the hogsheads continued . . . for the time being.

But now Casca had a problem.

He had arms—two cutlasses, a dirk, four pistols and one blunderbuss—and he had a boat, or at least access to a boat. But there were still hours until darkness, and it would not be possible to wait that long. Within the hour the sloop would be ready for the hawsers to be passed. When the shore party didn't appear . . .

Casca cursed his luck. If only the boatswain hadn't screwed things up. To get so close and lose it was hell. He was standing behind the screen of underbrush watching the sloop, and his men were beside him. None of them had interfered with the flight of the slaves. Let the poor bastards have the island.

"Aye, laddie. 'Tis partly right ye wair." The one-armed Scot was standing beside Casca, apparently holding no malice for the clubbing Casca had given him. "But, now. Aye dinna ken how we get to yon ship."

Hell, man, I don't either, Casca thought. He had figured on this thing being either spread out, with another boat from the sloop coming to investigate, or it being a case of the disappearance of the first mate and the opportunity to swim out to the sloop in the night darkness and come aboard. Now niether of these was going to happen. At the moment he didn't know what to do.

CHAPTER TEN

There just wasn't any damn way to get to the sloop. There it lay, anchored just at the edge of the shoal water, a couple of hundred yards offshore. Tantalizing. Might just as well be a thousand miles away. Damn!

Julio came out of the bushes, and the men grinned. The fairy London artist apprentice had made Julio's hair up into a pretty recognizable feminine style, particularly with the big white flower tucked in it. He had even done something with the face. What, Casca could not tell, but it apparently involved coconut oil and maybe just a touch of reddish-brown mud.

But it was the boobs that took the prize. Two halves of coconut meat—how the hell he had gotten the shell off without breaking the hemisphere of white meat inside Casca would have asked if he had not had other things on his mind. The two white half balls were tied

around Julio's chest with skinned vines to blend in with
Julio's own flesh, and then the coating of coconut oil
and reddish-brown mud had been used to blend it all in
and to tone down the white of the coconut and the
skinned vines to a more natural flesh color. The fairy
had even stuck one small berry into each coconut half
to make a teat. Close up, of course, you could tell—but
forty feet away the effect was startling.

Even the skirt, a coat turned inside out and tied
around Julio's hips with the navel showing, was be-
lievable attire.

Julio was reaching for the vines to get out of the
thing when Casca stopped him.

"Wait."

Julio's face held a question and so did that of the men
who now looked at Casca.

Hell! he thought, I don't have any better idea than
you do, but I've got to do something.

"We lure other men off the ship now, Captain
Long?" Julio asked in Spanish.

"Well . . . Hold it for a minute."

The captain of the sloop would certainly have a
spyglass. Besides . . .

"Halloo . . ."

The cry from the ship was slightly muffled, probably
because a slight crosswind had sprung up. Casca saw
there were clouds on the horizon. A storm? But that
wouldn't help him.

"Halloo! Halloo the beach!"

Maybe they wouldn't be able to identify the voice.
Casca cupped his mouth with his hands and yelled
back:

"Halloo!"

"Stand by to take strain!"

What the hell did that mean?

"Tell him 'Hawser's secure,' " the one-armed Scot growled.

Casca yelled the message.

They waited.

The two long thick ropes that lay on the beach, coming out of the water and leading back to the trees, began to move.

"Windlass on ship will take strain, help pull ship over on its side," Julio explained to Casca in Spanish, apparently thinking the scar-faced one did not know much about seamanship. The hawsers were straightening now, and Casca could see that the tide was also coming in, the water rising up the beach.

"Mister . . . Jenkins . . . !"

As the ship moved slowly sideways and came in closer the halloo became louder and more distinct.

Jenkins. That must be one of the officers. But which one? They had their first man trussed up with vines, his mouth gagged with leaves. The second one was dead, of course. But there was something else. Apparently the base of the trees was not visible from the sloop, hence the unconcern about seeing the shore party.

"Mister . . . Jenkins . . ."

Casca had to chance it. "Halloo!" But he turned his head slightly to the side, to blur his voice.

The sloop was both floating and being pulled rapidly nearer. Now a different voice came from the ship, much stronger now that the ship was closer to shore.

"Jenkins! Vere d' hell vas you?"

"Found spring. Set water detail."

"Vater? Vater? Jenkins, vas you dronk?"

The inspiration hit Casca then. He lifted his head and bawled: "Aye, Captain! Drunk as a lord!"

By now the sloop was scraping over the shoal edge. But the noise of her grounding was eclipsed by the torrent of Dutch profanity that now poured from the captain.

"Coom bock aboard, Mister Jenkins! At der vunce!" All motion of the sloop ceased. "Ver der hell der men? Vat you do mit men?"

"Water, Captain! Sent the men for water. Every last man jack for water!"

"Vater! *Dumbkopf!*" Silence. Casca and his men waited.

There was a definite change in the wind.

"Any chance of it blowing offshore?" Casca asked the one-armed Scot.

"Naw. Nawt now." He pointed in the direction roughly of the fort.

"Ah!"

Casca gave the orders, and three of the pirates rushed off to obey. . . .

It had not been the best of days for the captain of the sloop. The second boat, commanded by the third mate, had barely been launched when the lookout called:

"Fire ashore!"

In fact, before the boat was fully beached, what had been a single plume of smoke by now was a rolling cloud of acrid white flowing like a lava stream before the changing but still fairly gentle wind. The last the captain saw of his third mate was his smoke-shrouded figure clambering out of the boat along with the four slaves who had rowed him ashore. Then the smoke was upon the sloop itself, a bitter, choking smoke. The captain cursed. The female slave who was beside him at the moment made the mistake of choking before he did, so he slapped her across the mouth.

There was confusion—but not for too long. The smoke was already beginning to thin, blown by a vagary of the shifting wind, when the boat came alongside the sloop. The second mate had just started the order to help its occupants aboard when they came of their own accord—men with clubs, a one-armed giant with a cutlass, and the scar-faced devil with a feather in his hat.

Pirates!

The captain drew his sword.

Casca was in no mood for any fancy footwork. He pressed the attack.

But, no matter what the failings of the sloop captain might be in other areas, he wasn't a bad swordsman. He gave Casca a run for his money. Long after the sloop was otherwise neutralized he was still battling Casca on the fantail—and holding his own.

Casca had had enough of this shit. He lunged hard and slashed, forcing the sword from the captain's hand. The fat Dutchman was now cornered at the taffrail. He looked about him, saw that his ship was taken, that Casca's men were in control and that Casca held the cutlass ready to kill him if he moved. It was all over.

But not quite.

On the other side of the deck the female slave cowered against the rail, eyes wide. The Dutch captain noted her, said something in Dutch that Casca could not understand, and suddenly yanked a belaying pin from the rail. The motion was too swift for Casca to stop, but the captain did not throw the pin at him. Instead he threw it, with all his force, full into the face of the female slave, smashing the right side of her cheek and her right eye. Screaming with pain she reached upward for her broken face, lost her balance, and toppled over the rail into the water below.

The fat Dutchman grinned and repeated whatever it was he had said before, and Casca guessed it was something on the order of ''If I can't have her you can't either.''

The son of a bitch!

He was smiling easily at Casca now.

Casca lowered the cutlass, turning the blade over as he did so, and then, very deliberately, thrust the sharp steel edge between the captain's legs and pulled up, reaching down with both hands to get a good leverage on the blade with the result that the cutlass sliced up through the captain's testicles, penis, lower gut, and came to rest momentarily on the fat Dutchman's breastbone.

There was no further need for the cutlass, so Casca pulled it out.

''Throw him overboard,'' he ordered to no one in particular. From the waters below, still hidden by the smoke, came a telltale commotion caused by sharks attracted to the bleeding female slave.

Suddenly there was a sound behind him. It warned Casca just in time. He whirled to face the one-armed giant Scot who was now swinging the other cutlass at his head. Casca got the picture immediately. The Scot had no intention of serving under him and was now taking this opportunity to rid himself of a rival.

But the knowledge did not do Casca all that much good. In turning he slipped on the blood gushing from the Dutch captain's stomach and went down.

And the Scot was upon him. . . .

CHAPTER ELEVEN

The Scot was a big man, and he had a long reach. When Casca slipped in the blood the cutlass overshot its mark, barely grazed the feather in Casca's hat, but it did strike down and bite into the aftrail. At the same time the Scot slipped in the same blood as Casca, skidded into him, and hit Casca's shoulders off balance, catapulting the big Scot over the rail. His reflex action made him let go of the cutlass, but that hand was not able to grab the rail in time—and that was the only hand he had. His body tilted momentarily on the rail, but the slanted deck had given him too much momentum. He slid over the side of the ship and into the clearing smoke that hid the hungry sharks below. They got him. . . .

Casca was for taking the sloop out to sea immediately. But there was the little matter of the incoming tide. They were now grounded on the edge of the shoal.

"Do we go ahead with the careening?" the fairy painter's apprentice asked. He was now the temporary third mate, appointed by Casca who had been impressed by the fairy's apparent education and good sense—and as a reward for setting up Julio as the lure.

"No." There was no point in worrying about the sloop's barnacles. They would either be able to take another ship or they wouldn't. The fine points didn't matter.

So far things had gone well. The burning of the fort that sent the cloud of smoke down had worked. Julio as the lure had distracted the third mate long enough for that operation to succeed. They had the ship. True, it was grounded, but when the tide reversed that would be taken care of. They even had some new recruits. Most of the black slaves had chosen piracy to freedom on the island. Casca had his reservations about the first mate who, untrussed, had said he wanted to join the pirates. The same went for the second mate. In both cases Casca had left the decision up to a council to be held once they were at sea. It was one of his few concessions to democracy—which was not exactly his favorite way of running things. There hadn't been any democracy in the legion.

"The tide is in. Do you want to warp the ship off?" Julio was at his elbow, a Julio back in man's clothing and with a grin on his face. Casca sensed that the young Spaniard had enjoyed the theatrics of playing a woman, though the reason why was a mystery to the scar-faced one. Every man to his own . . .

But, "warping the ship off". . . . What the hell was that? Casca had been on many ships—from Roman galleys to Spanish galleons—but he wasn't exactly the sailor type and he had difficulty remembering the techniques.

What saved him from answering was a yell from the top of the mast. One of the pirates, homesick apparently for a ship after years on the island, had climbed the mast. Now he yelled down:

"Sail ho! Two points on the starboard bow! Hull down!"

"Shall I have the anchor capstan manned to warp the ship off the shoal?" Julio asked Casca in Spanish, some of the technical terms unfamiliar to Casca's knowledge of the language.

But he saw what the young Spaniard was up to— telling him what to do without the embarrassment of coming right out with it. He wondered what the background of the young Spaniard was. The boy seemed to have training far beyond his years. And he was a bright boy, a very bright boy. As bright as Casca would have wanted his own son.

"She's a brig!"

Casca looked at the sky. The sun was low, but there was quite a lot of daylight left, even allowing for the fact that darkness always came suddenly in the tropics. There were clouds on the horizon aft, and the wind had shifted again slightly. Also, there was the sense of heaviness in the air that usually indicated a storm was coming. But it wasn't here yet, and there might still be time to try for the brig—plus there would be darkness in case they didn't cut it. So he gave the orders to drop the shore hawsers, to man the capstan, to pull on the anchor rope, and finally to set sail, the wind now being in a favorable position. There were still the hogsheads of sugar on deck, tilting the ship to one side, but there just wasn't time to do everything.

Somewhat to Casca's surprise the thing worked. The sloop came free and they slipped the anchor. It was all or nothing, Casca reminded himself, glancing again at the sky and seeing that there would be too much daylight to get away if the attack failed. So they made for the brig, the top of whose sails were now visible from the deck.

Casca ordered the cannon—there were only three of them—double-loaded with grape and tried to explain to his puzzled gunners how he wanted them fired. When they finally understood, one, a big American, objected.

"Aye," Casca agreed. "You're right. It might damage this old tub. But it ain't worth a damn to us anyway except to take this one ship." The words and the tone of voice did more to convince the American than the logic of it, but by that time the brig was clearly visible.

"Probably American built," the fairy third mate said. "They favor the hermaphrodite brig."

"Ten guns," Julio added in Spanish.

The two ships were closing fast—mainly because the brig was apparently a very fast sailer and very well handled. Trouble was they were going too close on what Casca had decided was the wrong side. He was just about to give an order to the helmsman when he saw the brig's sails open and her bow begin to turn. She had made it easier for him. He gave his helmsman a course opposite from what he had intended and changed the angle of his own sails. It worked. Instead of a head-on collision course the two vessels were now turning in unequal circles, the faster brig in a much larger one.

Now what?

CHAPTER TWELVE

Casca could see the brig bearing down on him, all sails set, but at a tack. She was very fast. His own sloop moved sluggishly, the barnacled hull dragging, the overbalanced side with the hogsheads making one tack very difficult.

"Board her to windward, Sir," Julio offered.

"Windward?"

"Yessir."

"Where the hell did you learn so much about tactics?"

"I was a royal cadet, Sir." Something had transformed the young Spaniard. The prospect of action had apparently thrown him back into another time. His manner was disciplined, military. Casca considered . . . Hell, maybe the kid knew what he was talking about.

"Windward. That would be hard to do with this slow tub."

"Ordinarily, yes Sir. But look! The color of the water there. That lighter color. Shoal water, Sir. He'll have to avoid that—unless he knows the waters here very well and it is deep enough for him to cross. But these shoals change all the time. I don't think he would risk it, Sir.''

The kid keeps using ''he''—in his mind it is a naval battle.

''Look, Sir! I'm right! She's shortening sail.''

The brig was coming under easy sail.

''Get on the weather quarter of her, Sir! Come within half a pistol shot!'' Excitement raced through the boy's voice, and his face glowed.

''All right,'' Casca decided. Go with the kid. ''Come about!'' he yelled. ''Make all sail!'' Maybe, with a little luck—''

Damn!

On the tack the weight of the hogsheads canted the sloop far over, but, oddly, that very angle seemed to help. The old ship was slicing through the water like a live thing.

''I'd suggest, Sir, you lay on board on the weather side, either exactly abreast or a little abaft.'' Julio's voice was now crisp, cool, and he was standing rigidly beside Casca as if to belie the excitement in his dark brown eyes. A warmth came over Casca, a warmth greater than the heat of the tropic sun that was beaming full down now that the shadow of the sail had shifted away on this tack. Julio. Like a son. That he could have a son like this. . . .

They were closing fast. Out of Casca's side vision he saw one of his gunners reach for a slow match.

''Don't fire until I give the order!'' he bellowed, first in English, then again in Spanish. ''And in platoon!'' Damn! He couldn't think of the Spanish word for platoon.

Julio grinned. *''Unísonancia?''* he offered.

"That'll do," Casca agreed, and roared the order that they should fire in unison on his command. Probably shake the sloop to pieces, but what was the difference? Good for only this one battle anyway. All, or nothing at all.

They were within range. The next few moments would tell the story. Casca could see the black muzzles of the brig's cannon trained on him. She was a ten-gun brig. They would have to run the gauntlet of the five cannon on this side. Now! . . . No. . . . The brig was holding fire for some unknown reason.

So that was it!

The brig had been flying no colors. Now the Jolly Roger broke from her mast. Through the brass spyglass, Casca could see the enemy captain also watching him with a spyglass. Careful son of a bitch. Wanted to make damn sure he knew who I was before he committed himself. Careful . . . That was a useful thing to know about an enemy.

Casca caught the slight movement of the spyglass away from the other man's eyes.

"Take cover!" he roared immediately and saw his men drop behind the hogsheads as he had arranged. Only he, Julio, and the helmsman were left standing.

Casca started to order the boy to hit the deck, but it was too late.

The brig fired, a rolling volley beginning with the forward cannon and stepping raggedly back toward the stern.

One . . . Two . . . Three . . . Four . . . Five . . .

All five cannon had fired before the first shot hit the sloop.

A ball. Into the bow. Low. Almost at waterline.

The second ball went into the galley, smashing wood, throwing deadly splinters. The jagged shards of broken timber slashed at the men in range. Screams. Blood. One man was impaled on a long sliver and pushed into the scuppers, his guts oozing out along the jagged edge of the bloody wood.

The third ball missed entirely, almost magically passing through the only clear space between sail and mast and stays without hitting anything.

The fourth hit admidships, smashing timbers close to the waterline, opening a hole—it would be wide enough to sink the sloop.

The fifth came a little abaft amidships, but higher than the fourth ball. Casca could feel the shock to the timbers. All his concern about protecting his men from grape had been for nothing. The brig meant to sink them.

Now!

"Stand by to fire! *Uno! Dos! Tres!*"

His cannon roared. Maybe not entirely in unison, but reasonably well timed for amateur gunners. A hail of grape poured into the deck of the brig, hidden now by the cloud of smoke.

"Grapnels!"

The ships were coming together. But—

"Look out, Sir!" Julio yelled. "She's bracing sharp aback her headsails!"

It was hard to see in the smoke, but the tips of the sails did show above the dark cloud from the burned powder. The brig was falling off, and even as Casca watched, the enemy sails aft began to square, to give her sternway.

"Put your helm a-weather!" Julio cried, forgetting the "Sir," and the helmsman obeyed even before

Casca could give the order, then looked guiltily at Casca, who smiled and nodded.

"Now, a-lee!"

The maneuver succeeded. The brig's last minute attempt to avoid contact failed. The two ships smashed together, aided actually by the present roll of the brig.

"Grapnels!" Casca repeated, and the two vessels were locked together. "Boarders away!"

Through the smoke he could hear a like order being given on the brig, almost like an echo of his own voice.

But then it was time to stop thinking and go to fighting. Cutlass in his right hand, Casca leaped over the gunwales and into the smoke aboard the brig.

Nothing gentle was going on aboard the brig Casca and his men had stormed. If they had thought this was going to be an easy fight they were sadly mistaken. What met them in the smoke and blood on the brig's deck were men every bit as deadly as they themselves. With one difference: the brig's crew were better armed. First there were the blasts of pistols and muskets. Then the flashing cutlasses against the clubs—and what few cutlasses and swords had been in the arms locker of the sloop or taken from its officers—of Casca's men.

But the brig crew had not expected such a maneuver as the boarding on that tack, nor had they expected Casca's savage blast of double-loaded grape fired in unison. Nor had they anticipated the animal-fierce charge of Casca's men. What they had thought was that they would board the little sloop. What they got was a confused, brutal, bloody battle. Casca's men knew they had only this one chance. Like pit bulldogs that went for the throat, Casca's men went first for the kill.

As for Casca, that scar-faced one had taken a lot of shit recently, and the battle was one way to get it out of his system. Nothing fancy, just swing . . . chop . . . cut . . .

He worked his way to the captain of the brig, a big, tough, bare-headed brute with coarse coal-black hair who had just emptied a brace of pistols into the men on either side of Casca and now dropped them and reached for his cutlass.

What got Casca's attention was that the captain immediately went into the second position of the Naval Cutlass Exercise, legs angled out, proof that he must have had some British Navy experience.

Apparently he did. The son of a bitch knew what he was doing. Casca's blade clashed on his. Cut. Thrust. Parry.

But by now the battle was almost over, and Casca's men were taking the ship, though at terrific losses. After parrying one blow, Casca saw out of the extreme edge of his vision one of the brig crew leaving the battle and heading for the captain's cabin aft. There was something about this one that briefly caught his attention, probably because the brig crewman was so slender. Yet he had fought—from what little Casca had seen—brilliantly. However, he did not have an opportunity to go into the matter since at that moment the bare-headed captain suddenly pressed the attack.

Casca parried. He was getting tired. And the suppressed anger that had been in him ever since that morning in McAdams' compound boiled back up. The hell with this! He slashed savagely at the captain, recovered immediately, and again pressed the attack. Somewhere in the parry move by the captain Casca's blade slid off the other's and sliced away the captain's ear, which surprised that worthy to no end, a rather fatal mistake since Casca immediately took advantage of the captain's momentary confusion to pull back his cutlass and sweep it again forward, slicing halfway through the captain's neck. Blood spouted from the half-severed stump, a fountain whose outer edges sprayed toward Casca, and, though he immediately jumped back, a thin film of the dying man's blood salted his lips.

But the battle was over. Casca's blow was the last of the fight. They had the brig. Casca looked at his men—what was left of them. He had lost at least a third, but there were still enough hands to man the brig. Julio, who had come up beside him, was grinning with elation.

"A fine victory, Sir!" he said in Spanish. "You did—"

Whether Casca saw the movement in the bottom part of the rigging out of the corner of his eye or whether it came totally unexpectedly he never really knew. But there was movement. And a pistol shot. A dying brig crewman who had been posted in the rigging, probably with a musket or two, had fired one ball in the last seconds of his life. He had sighted on the large-framed man with the scar on his face.

Casca was knocked off his feet. For a blink of time he thought someone had coldcocked him again. Then he heard the report of the musket and saw Julio spin around and hit the deck. Switching his eyes to where the shot had come from, he saw the shooter let loose of the rigging and fall into the sea.

Scrambling over to Julio he rolled the boy over to his back. A deep sigh of relief went through him. He wasn't hurt bad. The slug had only taken out a piece of meat the width of a man's thumb from his left arm. Dumb kid had seen the crewman taking aim and thrown himself in front of Casca to protect him. An exercise in futility but Julio didn't know that.

He gave the rest of his motley crew orders to do what they could to make ready for sail. They did as they were bade and set about it. Fortunately there wasn't much structural damage. Their own grape shot had killed men but had done little harm to the ship itself. And they worked together—Brotherhood men, Spaniards and black ex-slaves—though the truth of the matter was that it was the calming influence of the London fairy that was responsible for the harmony of the moment. He seemed to understand emotions— good or bad—better than the others.

As they worked Casca washed and bandaged Julio's arm and left him to rest in the shade beside the cook shack and went below to inspect his prize.

He was met at the bottom by the castaway he had appointed first mate who nodded his head down the hallway to the captain's quarters and mumbled:

"We got a problem."

"What?"

"Somebody in the captain's cabin. Door's locked. We coulda broke it down, but we thought you . . ." He left the rest of it unsaid.

But when Casca went down the passageway to the captain's cabin, a ship's lantern in his hand against the darkness, and tried the cabin door it was no longer locked. Behind him the first mate shrugged. "It was locked when we came down." The lantern light shone on the faces of the two pirates behind the first mate, ship's axes in their hands. Casca turned back to the cabin door and opened it.

A large lamp, swinging in gimbals, lit the cabin brightly. Directly under it, trussed securely to the captain's chair and with a green baize gag in his mouth, was the retarded giant Casca had first met at McAdams' compound.

In the shadows to the giant's left, holding two cocked pistols pointed directly at Casca's stomach, stood a redheaded woman.

"Hold it right there, Scarface. Take one more step and I'll fill your stinking gut with lead."

CHAPTER THIRTEEN

"Katie Parnell?"

"Aye." She smiled. "Oh, hell. The Katie belongs to me. The Parnell I got off a tombstone. It's a long story—and not one I'm going to tell you."

The two of them were sitting at the table in the captain's cabin, one on either side, the big giant—still trussed and still gagged—at the head of the table, his eyes watching Casca and the redheaded woman. There was nobody else in the cabin. Casca had sent the first mate and the two seamen away—not something that pleased the first mate who had taken one look at the woman and her two pistols and then looked at Casca, the mate's eyes plainly saying that this was a hell of a way to run a ship. But he and the two seamen had gone. The woman had then produced a bottle of wine from the liquor locker, casually laying both pistols on the table as she did so. Indicating the table, she had extracted the cork from the bottle with a practiced hand, taken a healthy swig while still standing, and then sat down and slid the bottle across to Casca, all the time completely ignoring the big giant at the head of the table.

Casca was amused. Very few women he had ever known had behaved anywhere near this way, and there was a kind of good-natured mockery in Katie's eyes that seemed to say she took everything in life as a game to be played for the fun of it only. Coming as Casca did from treating Julio and the emotional draining of the battle—no matter how many times he fought there was always that dark feeling afterward—the strange redhead was a welcome relief. The fact that she was a pretty good-looking woman and the wine was first-rate—reminiscent of the Falernian of his youth—also helped matters.

He grinned. "Off a tombstone?"

"Off a tombstone. Now, who the hell are you?"

She was tall for a woman. Even sitting at the table her eyes were on a level with his, and her build was athletic; Casca realized with surprise that she had been the crewman he had seen leave the battle and go toward the captain's cabin. She had fought, then, alongside the men. And if he needed proof, he saw when she moved her arm the dried blood on the leather sleeve. She must be pretty good. He knew his men.

But she was also a woman. The waistcoat had the bulges in the right locations, and when she leaned over the table for the bottle, not asking him for it, but merely leaning over and taking it, he could see down the wide opening of her shirt the obvious contours of her breasts—not big cowlike boobs but the interesting kind that made one want to coddle her.

"Who are you?" she repeated. "I thought I knew all the Brotherhood captains. Are you new to the business?"

"Yes."

"You got a fucking name?"

The way she said it was . . . well . . . different. Neither the word nor the kind of explosive rat-a-tat-tat spacing of her speech was what one might expect from a lady of quality. On the other hand the kind of impish amusement in her changeable eyes—they were either gray or brown depending on the way the light hit them—and the impression she gave that life was the laughing joke of a child made any tagging of her as an ordinary whore out of the question. She was simply . . . something different.

"Name," she repeated. "You got to have your pump primed? Ain't you never seen no woman before?"

That did it. Casca grinned. He looked at her and spoke solemnly:

"Methinks the laddy doth protest too much."

She threw her head back and roared with laughter, and with her head back there was a graceful sweep to her neck. A mature woman, but a young one. Maybe twenty-four. Maybe twenty-five.

She stopped the laugh as quickly as it had begun, but the merriment was still in her eyes. "Shakespeare! Forsooth the man hath read Shakespeare! A pirate captain who quotes Shakespeare! Scarface, art thou the Bard of Avon come back to life to ride the waves 'neath the Jolly Roger? Is thy name William?"

Casca didn't know what the hell she was talking about, and the thought that maybe she was making fun of him pissed him off a little. He said sourly: "Captain Cass Long." Then to play whatever game she had started with the words: "At your service, ma'am."

Her eyes again glinted with the impish light. "And I

bet your service would be fucking good, too, Captain Long. Only I do not intend to be serviced at the moment. You have missed the rutting season, Scarface.''

Casca had had enough of it. ''Who the hell are you, anyway? And why have you got him tied up?'' He pointed toward the big giant.

''Oh, him.''

''Where did you get him?''

''We fished him out of the water. Around dawn. He was hanging onto a hatch cover.''

''You tie up everybody you fish out of the water?''

''I do if I remember seeing him at the Governor's Palace in Virginia. I think he's a spy for Governor Spotiswoode.''

''Spy?'' That had been Blackbeard's excuse for marooning him. What was going on here?

''Yes''

''And what were you doing in the Governor's Palace in Virginia?'' Where was Virginia, anyway? Was that the colony just above Charles Town? Casca wasn't too sure of his geography.

''And wouldn't you like to know, Captain Cass Long—or whatever your name is, Scarface.''

''He's no spy.''

''How do you know?''

''He was McAdams' bodyguard.''

''What? How do you know that?''

''We were on Blackbeard's ship together. Going to meet Tarleton Duncan.''

''Ah!'' She thought about that for a moment, then got up, went to the giant, took a dirk from the sheath at her waist, cut his ropes, and pulled the gag from his mouth. ''If you know McAdams, then whatever you say is okay. But this one here . . . he seemed a little odd.''

Casca tapped his own forehead. "Sometimes a belfry doesn't carry a full set of bells.''

She looked puzzled. Then she understood. "Ah!''

Casca did not tell her he was certain that the giant only pretended to be retarded. Instead he said: "But he's an excellent fighter.''

"Is he now? Then what was he doing floating on a hatch cover in the middle of the ocean?''

"I don't know. Ask him.''

"I did. Without satisfaction.'' Suddenly her eyes narrowed and she turned back to Casca. "McAdams. Tarleton Duncan. If you were on your way with Teach to meet Tarleton Duncan, then what are you doing captaining such a ragtag and bobtail crew? And with such a miserable excuse for a ship?''

Casca grinned.

He gave her own words right back to her.

"And wouldn't you like to know, Katie Parnell, or whatever your name is?''

That's when the storm hit, the storm that had been brewing all day. Whatever Casca might have found out from Katie—or she from him—had to be put aside when the first blast of the gale force wind nearly threw the brig on her beams. Then came the thunder, lightning, torrential rains, high seas and gusting winds. They fought the storm for most of the night, the brig pitching and rolling, plowing her bow under the invincible waves, rolling so far abeam that the yardarms would have pointed at the sky had the sky been visible. And all in pitch blackness.

Less than an hour before dawn the storm suddenly

ceased—or they had waddled out of it—as quickly as it
had hit, and in the ragged gray opening torn in the sky a
full moon shone. By daylight even the sea was calm,
and the following day was perfect, the brig gliding
gently over a blue sea touched occasionally with tiny
whitecaps from a soft breeze.

And it stayed that way for days. A pirate's life? This
was more like a vacation at sea—or more likely an
outing for women on an inland lake. Casca didn't
complain. Hell, a man took what he could get. He
would ride with it.

Of course, one ride he did not get. Katie Parnell
could take care of herself, and though Casca felt he
would eventually bed her, that pleasant state of affairs
did not come to pass—yet. Nor did he really learn who
Katie was. He got hints. What he put together seemed
to be that Katie's mother had been the mistress of some
important man in the colonies—somebody very high
up—and this man had been Katie's father. She knew a
hell of a lot about government at the top level. And she
apparently knew a hell of a lot about some other things,
too. But what was she doing in the Brotherhood? All
Casca could get out of her was the implication that, as a
woman, she would never be allowed to use her talents
in the respectable world, but as a pirate she could be
whatever she was damn well capable of being. But
whether this was the truth or not he could not tell. Katie
liked to lie—when it was just for the fun of it. She was
certainly not your normal everyday woman.

But she was a source of information. Casca learned
more about pirates and piracy talking to her than he had
so far being one himself. For one thing, the business of
the Brotherhood was just that—business. Almost all

the pirates had connections, those that didn't didn't stay in the trade very long. Many were "silent partners" to merchants ashore. Sometimes a cargo of sugar, adroitly handled by the merchant ashore, returned more gold to the pirate than the capture of a Spanish "treasure ship." And there was connivance in high places. Governor Eden of North Carolina apparently made no bones about his associations—even to the point of attending one of Blackbeard's "weddings."

It was at the mention of Blackbeard's weddings that Katie came closest to acting like a woman—or rather showing a woman's anger. Blackbeard, she said, had been married more than a dozen times—fifteen, sixteen, nobody knew the exact number of times—and each time to a young girl, usually in her midteens. What made Katie furious was the fact that on each wedding night after Blackbeard had enjoyed the girl as long as he wished, he would then call in his officers and turn the girl over to them—five, six, however many it happened to be—and they would use her for the rest of the night. Nice people, these pirate captains. And what did she know about Tarleton Duncan?

The expression on her face grew thoughtful, and, since she was standing with Casca at the rail of the ship, she looked out toward the far horizon.

"I don't really know what it is that created the whispers about Tarleton Duncan. In fact, I don't know what the whispers are, though I suspect it's because I'm a woman that nobody tells me. But there's something. Something odd . . ."

Casca had to leave it at that.

What really got him, though, was Katie's assertion

that most pirates weren't odd. Casca just happened to have known the oddest, Blackbeard. Most captains were pretty ordinary men.

"Prove that," Casca challenged her.

"Well, take Stede Bonnet. Major Stede Bonnet. Just an ordinary bored man. He was living off 500 pounds a year in real estate in Barbados. On the quiet, and because he was bored, he fitted out a sloop from that island so he could become a pirate. He wasn't too competent, and even though the ship belonged to him personally, the crew put in under the command of one of his foremast men, a certain Edward Teach."

"Blackbeard?"

"Yes. Though that name came later."

"But they still operate together."

"Oh, yes. It's a business, you see, Scarface."

"Just ordinary people."

"Just ordinary people."

But the giant he had traveled with from McAdams' compound was not "ordinary people." Or was he?

It was a day or so before Casca could talk to him alone.

"What the hell were you doing in the water?"

"Accident. I was trying to steal a boat, and in the darkness I fell overboard."

"Steal a boat?"

"To come to your aid."

"Mine?"

"When Blackbeard marooned you, I thought it was because you were a spy for Woodes Rogers."

"Aye? Well, now . . ."

"Why did you vouch for me?"

"Shit, man, everybody to his own business."

"And you don't care that I'm—"

"In the pay of the governor of Virginia? That's your business, fellow."

"And your business?"

"What I contracted with McAdams for—to get his niece. And then get my ass to the mainland."

"But you've got a ship of your own now. Why not just go to Charles Town yourself?"

"I thought of that."

"And?"

"Bastards like McAdams have a lot of connections. I might get to the mainland faster by doing his little job—which should not be too hard to do."

"You think so."

Casca shrugged.

"But you're officially a pirate yourself now. If you're caught you could be hanged."

"That's true."

The giant was quiet for a moment, then he said:

"You know something, Cass Long?"

"What?"

"I overheard part of your conversation with the woman about which pirates were odd and which were not. The thing is, Cass Long, you're the odd one."

Casca smiled and started to respond, but at that moment he saw two of the Spanish pirates standing by the foremast engaged in what was obviously a very, very private conversation, and the smile left his face.

So far there had been no trouble among the Spaniards, the Brotherhood men, the three remaining black slaves, and those of the crew of the brig who still lived.

He hadn't been around men who had the potential for explosion for nothing. He knew he might be sitting on a powder keg.

And probably was . . .

But before he had too much time to worry about it something else happened.

''Sail ho! Two points off the starboard bow!'' The lookout's voice came down clear and excited from the mast.

And Casca knew that shortly he would be in pursuit of his first prize as a pirate.

CHAPTER FOURTEEN

The chase was a brigantine under easy sail, flying before the wind. Casca ordered the brig about, and they went for the brigantine that continued on course, showing no sign that she feared an attack—more likely, confident she could outrun them. But with only a few minutes sailing on the new tack it was obvious that Casca's ship was overtaking her. Big Jim, who was now Casca's aide as a deterrent to those of his crew who had shown any desire to heave their makeshift captain over the side, halted by Casca and eyed the brigantine shrewdly for a few moments.

"She's got good lines. If she puts on more sail she'll show us her heels."

At this point there was nothing to do but go for it, though Casca didn't like the feel of it at all. But if he didn't at least make the effort his own crew would probably haul his ass back to the island and throw him off again.

Still he'd been sucked into too many ambushes not to be wary. . . .

When he put the spyglass to his eye and searched her

decks, she seemed innocent enough. The helmsman was at the wheel, the master—or mate—on the fantail beside him, the crew at their guns.

Might as well go in for the attack.

That, however, brought up some problems. As far as Casca could tell the chase was flying no flag. She might be a pirate ship like his own—or she might simply be a merchantman, a coastal trader. If she were merchant, what nation? Spanish, and no one would give a damn. But English or American, and he was deliberately committing an act of piracy for which he could be hanged.

And for which Katie Parnell could be hanged, too.

Hell! Casca thought, how do I get myself involved in these situations?

But the biggest problem was, if he did attack, how in the hell did he go about starting the action? There were times when Casca regretted that he did not have more sea experience. He could see that they were gaining on the prize, but he wasn't sure just what to do next. Slide up beside her and board? But which side?

"Make up your mind, Scarface."

Katie had come aft and was standing beside him.

"What?"

"About boarding him."

"Aye . . ."

"Don't know what to do, do you? Look, you're close to the wind. Board him to leeward."

"What do you know about sailing a ship?"

"A damn sight more than you do. If I hadn't had the bad luck to be born a woman, I'd be a damn better captain than Blackbeard ever will be."

Casca looked at her and grinned. Wearing the floppy high boots of Russian leather, dark blue knee britches, a man's linen shirt and a Turkish vest with a brace of pistols slung on a wide sash, a cutlass in the hanger at her hip, and wearing a burger's brimmed hat with a feather in the band, she sure as hell didn't look like any woman. More like a first mate. Or captain. And that intent face. Except for the lack of beard it could be the face of any man eager for combat.

"Well," she said, "are you going to give the orders, or are you going to stand there and stare at me like some tongue-tied schoolboy?"

When he didn't answer immediately, she bellowed, "Port your helm two points! All borders! Standing by to board to leeward! Gunners! Prime your fucking guns!" She gave Casca a sweet smile, then added, "Captain's orders! And lively, lads, lively. Or the captain will have your stinking guts for garters!"

A nudge at his elbow brought him around to see Julio standing beside him, a painful expression on his face. It wasn't caused by his wound, which was healing nicely, but by the usurption of his place as Casca's advisor in matters of the sea. It was plain to see he was a bit jealous of the defiant, vulgar bitch who stood by Casca's side and shouted orders in his name. Casca gave Julio a brisk hug, careful not to further damage his wound and whispered in his ear, "Don't worry, you know how women are. She's just showing off. You take a place aft till we get ready to board. And don't cross over with the first group; you're still going to be a bit stiff for any brisk sword play. Now go on." Julio did as he was bade, still a bit miffed but feeling better.

Katie stuck her tongue out at him and turned back to the business at hand. Casca had to admit she was a hell of a lot better at it than he was. He should have been pissed off, but instead he was just amused. It was impossible to get mad at Katie. Grinning, he said, just loud enough for her to hear, "If diddling your ass is as much fun as listening to you, I've got something to look forward to."

"You've got something to look forward to, all right, Scarface, but it ain't boorading my ass. I decide who I bundle and who I don't, and your name ain't on the list right now."

"So—"

"Dammit, Scarface, you're in pistol range! Ease off a point or you'll be raked by his waurter swivel before any of our guns can be brought to bear!"

She was right. He gave the order to the helmsman.

"Now come up with him, but edge away a little round aft." The helmsman didn't wait for Casca to relay the command; he knew who was giving the orders.

Casca didn't care as long as she was right. "You just do as you please, madam."

He was being sarcastic, but she took him literally—or at least pretended that she did. "All right, now. Come close upon his lee quarter—close enough so that your cathead almost touches him. You do know what a cathead is, don't you? Those large timbers projecting out of the side of the ship forward where your anchor is secured. Or, if you're still the bleedin' farm boy I think you are, the part of the ship that looks like the horns of a cow." Now she was grinning.

Damn, but he liked her style.

"Let's get this fighting over with so we can start—"

"Look out! You'll go too far ahead! Haul your sheets well aft! Put your helm hard a-lee! Let the head sheets fly!"

Damn! The woman was a real sailor. Casca gave the

orders. They were executed, and the brig shivered her sails and closed the prize side by side.

"Gunners! Fire!" Casca ordered, this time without any coaching from Katie.

"Hell!" she said to him. "I figured you knew about guns and—" The rest was drowned in the thunder of their broadside, grapeshot at point-blank range sweeping the deck of the prize.

"Grapnels!" Casca ordered.

A moment later, in the dense black smoke from the guns, the two ships came together. The grapnels were thrown, the two hulls lashed.

"Boarders!" Casca ordered, and, cutlass in hand, leaped for the other deck, Katie beside him, her own cutlass at the ready.

Both teetering on the gunwale at the same time, momentarily halting.

"There's something wrong, Scarface," she muttered. "Why didn't he fire on us?"

There wasn't time for him to answer. He jumped aboard the prize, Katie Parnell matching him step for step, and for the first time in his life Casca Rufio Longinus felt the odd pleasure of going into battle with a woman he trusted. . . .

Whether he or Katie were the first of the boarders or not he could not tell since the heavy smoke covered the entire ship. His feet were now on the deck of the brigantine. A quick glance upward did not show anyone in the rigging, at least not within his limited sight. Odd . . . the captain of the brigantine must have his head in his ass. A couple of men in the rigging with blunderbusses could play hell with boarders.

"Too quiet, Scarface," Katie muttered.

She was right. It was definitely too quiet—and boarders should have been met at the gunwales. Casca smelled ambush.

"Watch your ass, Katie," he growled.

The smoke was clearing.

The yells up forward scared the shit out of him. Confused yells. His own men.

"What—"

Whatever it was Katie was going to say, she never said it—and Casca saw why.

The clearing smoke, blown forward from the bow so that he and Katie were the last to see the clearing, suddenly showed the helmsman and the mate—neither more than a cutlass swing away.

The helmsman was old for a sailor, or at least the white hair and sunken cheeks seemed to say so. As for the mate, his salt-encrusted beard made it difficult to say whether he was young or old.

Actually, though, the age of the two men made no difference at all. Both were dead. Long dead. Dried, dressed corpses with a faint suggestion of a green slime. The wheel held the helmsman upright; the binnacle—where he was apparently standing when he died—held up the mate.

Standing beside him, Julio grabbed Big Jim's arm and pointed to the dead men. Big Jim said it for him. "Ghost ship!"

Others in the boarding party took up the cry and added to it: "Plague! It's a plague ship!" Casca could hear the confused cries in English and Spanish that had come from up forward. In the clearing smoke he could see his men jumping back aboard the brig, slashing free the ropes of the grappling hooks in a frantic haste to get free of the death ship.

"Look what the cannon did," Katie said quietly. The grape had smashed into the paper dry corpses and scattered parts of the bodies all over the forward deck, oddly missing the fantail where he and Katie were. But it was all dry; there was no blood.

"C'mon," he said. "Let's get off this thing." But they had waited too long. The brig was free and coming about, the gap of churned water between the two ships rapidly widening.

Calling to them to put about, his crew ignored him. There was no one nor anything worth returning to a plague ship for. The four of them stood there watching their brig put miles between them as the rigging and sails overhead began to flap with the increase of the winds. The storm was coming and they were trapped on a death ship. Julio made the sign of the cross and Big Jim moved to where the dead man stood by the helm and touched the dried husk on the shoulder. It fell to the deck and Big Jim took its place with a resigned look on his face.

The four of them waited not wanting to go below decks. As they each stood with their thoughts the skies darkened and the winds built even higher. The sea turned gray and the horizon was lost to sight. Only the black immensity of rolling cloud and rising wave joined them.

The wind gusted and with a loud crack that startled their minds back into activity, the fore-and-aft mainsail, its rigging probably weakened by hits from the grapeshot, suddenly collapsed and the brigantine was taken aback. The sudden motion threw Katie and

Casca to the deck. Julio found himself hanging next to a dried, grinning corpse. Then it was gone, blown over the side into the darkened sea. They were alone now; there were only the four of them, the ship, and the rising sea.

Aboard the brig which had been the late captaincy of Captain Cass Long, the discussion had now ended. As best the officers could tell, and since no one could recall seeing them, Captain Cass Long and Katie Parnell had been lost at sea, lost overboard when the brig separated from the ghost ship. That meant the brig was now without a captain, and the factions aboard her were ready to go at each other's throats—as soon as the storm was over. But they were in the storm, and since they couldn't agree on any of the stronger officers as captain, they finally chose the London fairy as acting captain, a choice which, no sooner made, was suddenly realized to have been the best damn thing they had ever done. He happened to be the only individual on the ship who seemed to have the ability to get along with all factions. Besides, he was a damn good seaman, and a good seaman was what they needed at the moment, the storm being what it was. . . .

"You still alive, Katie?"

"Hell, no, Scarface, I died hours ago."

"Thy voice, Katie dear, is not exactly that of an angel."

"Never was, Scarface. Never was."

Casca and she had lashed themselves to the binnacle after first lashing the wheel in place and so had ridden out the storm. Now it was dawn. The winds had died. The sea was moderating.

Casca got his lashings free and started to help Katie, but she had already freed herself. "One thing I'll never like," he growled good-humoredly, "is a damn woman who is as good as a man."

"Quit playing with the truth, Scarface. I'm the first woman you ever met as good as a man. There never was anybody else before. And, besides that, I'm better."

"Modest, aren't you?"

"Humility is not one of my vices, Scarface." She looked down the deck, the length of the ship, and grinned. "Well, we got scrubbed down real good."

She was right. The storm had swept the deck as clear as a double gang with holystones. There was now no trace of the dead crew. Except for the damage done by the volley of grape in their attack, the broken spar and crumpled mainsail, and a few other tattered and weathered sails here and there, the ship looked to be in excellent condition. Big Jim and Julio had been hard at work cleaning up as best they could. Big Jim cast the bodies to the deep while Julio said prayers for them. Between them they had cleared the deck of most of the wreckage from the fallen mast and sail.

Kate cast a professional eye over their domain. "It's not going to be easy to handle this thing with just the four of us. If we run into any more weather we might as well just go below and wait it out because we won't be able to do a damn thing about it.

Casca nodded knowing he was out of his depth. Julio had brightened up a bit and was hard at work scavenging in the cook shack. He'd gotten a fire started in the iron cook stove. At any rate they'd have some hot food. Big Jim was at the helm doing the best he could to keep with the wind so they'd make some headway, but he had no idea of where they wanted to go or what course to take. That was up to Kate. He wasn't a navigator. She gave him a heading that would take them into the main shipping lanes and in the general direction of Jamaica.

Casca poked through a pile of rubbish and grumbled: "Wonder what killed the crew. Whatever it was got all of them and it looks like at about the same time."

"Odd," Katie said thoughtfully.

"There's something else odd, too," Casca said, looking down the deck.

"What?"

"The hatches."

"Nothing odd about that, Scarface. They're battened down as they should be. The men were at the guns. Obviously they expected a battle."

"Aye. But—"

"Oh! I see." She caught it before he had a chance to tell her. Now, that was the kind of woman he liked. "The forward hatch."

"Wide open." Followed by Katie, Casca started forward, but she stopped him at the first hatch.

"Let's see what kind of cargo she was carrying."

The hatch cover off, both peered over the coaming.

"Damn!"

"Uniforms!" she added.

The cargo hold under this hatch was stuffed with military uniforms—not boxed or crated, but baled. The scent of the wool was strong, but it also had an odd additional odor that Casca found familiar . . . the odor of some fruit . . . Persian? He could not quite remember.

The next compartment was filled with barrel after

barrel of gunpowder. The one after that had stacks of muskets.

Somebody was supplying an army. A revolution? It would make sense here in the tropics—the gunpowder and muskets—but not the woolen uniforms.

Again, coming from both cargo compartments, there was that odor, stronger now, so strong that it even overpowered the smell of the gunpowder.

"Somebody's been eating almonds," Katie said, sniffing the air. "Funny odor for a ship."

Now Casca remembered. *Misch-misch*. Sweet Persian apricots. They had pits that smelled of bitter almonds.

When they got to the open hatch, the smell was not quite as strong, but, then, the compartment had shipped a lot of water in the storm last night. Not enough, though, to wash away the evidence of what had happened.

"What do you make of it, Scarface?"

"The same thing you do. Sloppy stowage. They had a cargo of fruit of some kind here. Looks like peaches and smells like apricots—but that doesn't make sense because that's not the kind of fruit that grows around here. Anyway, whatever had spoiled—began to work like wine.

Together they retrieved the splintered board that was stuck in the ladder leading down into the compartment.

"Part of a crate. Got smashed." In the darkness at the bottom of the ladder, in the gooey mass of the fermented fruit, there were odd-looking containers. Bottles—but not like wine bottles. The last time Casca had seen anything like them was in a private laboratory of an alchemist two hundred years ago. The stupid bastard had been trying to turn lead into gold but had only managed to kill himself with the fumes from the damn stuff he had mixed up. But that was a long time ago. . . . .

"There's an address on the crate," Katie said, meaning the piece of wood.

It had been burned on, but it wasn't easy to read.

"Herr Doktor Stahl, Physician to His Majesty, King of Prussia, His Majesty's Palace, Berlin."

Katie read the look in his eyes. "What's wrong, Scarface?"

"Let's go see if there's a logbook in the captain's cabin."

There was a log, all right, but it was written in a language neither Katie nor Casca could read. Portuguese, Casca thought—and he was pretty sure he was right when they found the Portuguese flag, neatly folded in a cubbyhole of the captain's desk.

But it was the charts that confounded Casca.

"Portugal? Spain? You mean they were all the way over on the other side of the ocean?" Katie's voice was incredulous.

But that's what the charts said. The last marking on the chart . . .

As best Casca could guess something had happened in that forward compartment. Either the smashed medicines or alchemical supplies or whatever they were that were being carried to Dr. Stahl—or the rotting fruit—had created such a stink that the captain had opened the hatch to keep the odor out of the uniforms. Then there had been some kind of danger. Pirates? Anyway, while the men were at their stations, something had killed them. Killed them instantly. And the ship had been carried by the current south, far south, until the current turned west, and wind and current had carried the ship to the Americas. Must have taken a long time because the bodies had dried out to where they were like paper. That was why he had seen the helmsman at the wheel, the captain at the binnacle; their dried bodies were propped against these supports and apparently there had been no storms to dislodge them. There wouldn't have been if the current had carried them south.

But what had killed them? Poison? "We better not eat any of the food," he growled. He looked at the open hatch. Could the smell coming out of that have killed them? Shit! Casca had been in a lot of stinking places, and none of them had ever killed anybody that he knew of. "I wonder—"

"Save it, Scarface," Katie said quietly.

"What?"

"We got company."

He looked where she pointed, just off the port bow. There was a ship, hull up, on the horizon.

"If she holds that tack another quarter hour we'll be on a collision course," Katie said.

Damn!

CHAPTER SIXTEEN

Casca had Julio hoist the Portuguese flag, but there was damned little they could do against the ship now bearing down on them under full sail. She was a schooner, apparently a merchant ship, and she was flying British colors.

"Looks pretty," Katie murmured.

Casca eyed her, thinking, I'd forgotten she was a woman. But the schooner did make a nice picture, racing toward them at full speed, bow cutting the water and throwing a white spume against the blue sea, now so calm after the storm of three days past.

But pretty or not, the schooner could be a potential hazard. The English flag might be a ruse. If so, he and Katie would just have to play it by ear. For a second he regretted having tossed all the bodies overboard. They might have had the same effect on the schoonermen as they did on the other men from the brig.

The vessel showed no sign of reducing her speed or lowering any sail. She only veered off enough to pass within hailing distance. Close enough so that Casca could make out the figurehead of the schooner clearly, a freshly painted figure of a woman with feathered headdress and bare boobs with rosy nipples. And on the aft deck, the master stood with a hailing trumpet in his hands.

As they passed, the master's voice called out:

"Pirates! Pirates ahead!" And then called out, ". . . arleton . . . uncan!"

Either he had said "Tarleton Duncan!" or Casca had imagined it.

There had been a few crewmen lining the rail of the schooner, but not many. They were apparently not interested in Casca's ship. All they wanted to do was to get the hell out of there and into safer waters.

Then they were gone. Casca turned back to Katie, but she had a thoughtful look on her face. She was searching the horizon ahead, but it was empty. She looked back at the receding sails of the schooner. And then she headed for the hatch which led to the captain's quarters, taking her clothes off as she went. Julio averted his eyes at this brazenness. Big Jim just swallowed his Adam's apple.

"What the hell are you doing?"

"Get out of your clothes, Scarface. Now!"

"Why?"

"Because you've been wanting to diddle me ever since we met. And I think, dammit, I want to try you on for size right now. Besides if I know anything about that ship, we might be too busy to do it later. But right now we have time, so let's have at it." Casca thought about that for a moment.

"What the hell are you waiting for?" She was down to the buff, and damn if there wasn't a woman under all those men's clothes. Nice. Very nice. She had firm high breasts with nipples already hard and puckered from the sea breeze.

"You can look later," she complained. "Now get on with it, you clod!"

He did. Julio busied himself with whatever he could find to do. Sex was still an adventure yet to come for him. Big Jim just whistled a few bars of filthy sailor's songs and tightened his grip on the wheel.

The sight of his body—all the scars, all the evidence of past wounds—brought a puzzled look to her eyes.

"How did you get cut up like that?"

"It's a long story."

"Er . . ." She hesitated. "You still can . . ."

Casca laughed. "Hell, yes. Hell, yes!"

McAdams listened to the man's report and shook his head. Giving the wretch a few silver coins he sighed deeply. Well it was a long shot at best. Cass Long didn't get very far. Damn! Now he would have to think up another plan for the disposal of Duncan. God! The swine infuriated him. Who did Duncan think he was? If it had not been for McAdams' patronage the man would never have had his own ship. And now the dog turns on his master and bites the hand that fed him. Ingrates! The world is full of them.

McAdams sat in his woven cane chair on the veranda and looked out over his domain. It had taken years of labor and pain to acquire all that was now his and he hadn't gotten it by giving up anything. No, by the gods, he got where he was by taking. Duncan knew that. It was he, McAdams, that had first taken Duncan, when he was a wet-nosed pup, to sea with him. It was he who had taught him the craft of the sea raiders. For that was how McAdams had gained the foundation of his wealth. Always he had stayed in the shadows never letting his face be seen by those who survived a raid. It was Duncan he had put to the forefront and made captain of his own ship when he moved back to the island and became the principal broker for the Brotherhood. It was because of his management that Duncan, Teach and the others were rich men. He could have welded them into a major power.

But now! Duncan, that motherless pig, had outgrown his pants. McAdams had never interfered with Duncan's small pleasures. He understood them. But this recent betrayal was too much.

He called for rum punch from one of his male servants.

Duncan had grown greedy, wanting more, always more. Not only more of the money but of the power that was rightfully McAdams'. They had quarreled and McAdams had struck Duncan across the face.

Pride, McAdams thought. That was it. Duncan had too much pride and arrogance. It drove him to challenge McAdams for control. Since then Duncan had done his best to make McAdams' life miserable, undermining his authority at every chance. Now Duncan had taken something which was his and this he could not tolerate and many knew of it. If he didn't move and move fast his power would bleed away from him and so would his wealth. That he could not, would not let happen. . . .

Luck?

Casca wondered about that. Usually when something looked like luck it meant he was just about to get his ass in a sling. So maybe he shouldn't feel too good about the way it had worked out.

After he and Katie had bedded—and that had been pretty damn good, he had to admit—they had not encountered Tarleton Duncan as the British had warned. Instead, they had raised land. The luck part was that Katie recognized the coast, had been in the harbor, knew the town, and—more importantly—knew the waters. She had also spotted the *Scorpion* in port. It had not been easy bringing the ship around in a curving arc to approach offshore from a direction not visible from the town. And there was always the possibility that Tarleton Duncan had stationed a lookout on the point of land that rose up from the bay. But they had made it—and there had been no lookout. Duncan's men were apparently too busy raiding the town—a small trading village that had known this kind of thing before and was powerless to do anything about it.

It was not possible to do much with the ship. Anchoring was relatively easy. Getting away would be a different matter. They could cut the anchor rope, but unless they were lucky with tide and wind the ship would be useless to them. He and Katie might be able to manage a single sail—but that would be all. So, if they were unlucky, it would be the ship's smaller boat—the captain's gig—and the open sea.

Unless they lucked upon a fishing craft.

At the moment, Katie was in the gig below him. She, too, was dressed in one of the uniforms. And in the gig was the money chest from the captain's cabin, a small canister of gunpowder, several loaded muskets, and flint and steel. They were ready to board Duncan's ship.

The pirate standing gangway watch on the *Scorpion*

was, naturally, drunk—but not all that drunk. The apparition that he saw coming aboard made him blink his eyes. He had never seen such a gorgeous uniform—all dark wool and gold braid, gleaming medals hanging from colorful ribbons, a crimson sash, bright even in the dull light of the ship's lantern—and that enormous bearskin hat with its white feather plumes. What in hell!

"Captain Tarleton! And, by damn! step lively, lad, or . . ." The apparition whipped off into language that the pirate understood very well indeed.

"I don't know—" The pirate started to protest, but something in the icy depths of the pale blue eyes stopped him. He looked over the side. The apparition had come in a small gig, and there was another uniformed soldier—not nearly so gorgeous—at the oars. In the spilled light from the ship's lantern that single man was certainly no danger. Nor was the apparition armed except for the customary short sword any high-ranking son of a bitch would wear. The pirate nodded at a smaller companion. "Take him to the captain." The second pirate shrugged and started aft, Casca following.

The captain's quarters were protected by a closed door at which the pirate knocked. A big black man opened it—a man naked to the navel and with cold, hard eyes. Casca could not remember seeing such a giant since Jubala, the Numidian he had fought in a Roman arena long, long ago.

He asked for the captain. It was obvious that the pirate was afraid of the black man but did not want to show it. The black giant said nothing, only held the door wider for Casca, and when the scar-faced one was inside the companionway, the bearskin hat's plumes brushing the overhead, he closed and bolted the door. The silence in the companionway was uncanny. The area must be relatively soundproof. And if the other doors were as thick as this one . . . Casca began to worry. But he had no choice now. He was committed.

The giant led him down the companionway to another door. Before it was a small space, a tiny square room made by offsets set into the walls on either side and lighted by a ship's lantern hung in gimbals from the overhead. There was a small, hard bench in the offset on either side of the door. The giant pointed to one of the benches.

"Wait," he mumbled, his voice soft and slurred as though he were mouthing soft mud. "Captain busy."

Casca had no intention of waiting for anybody, but he moved as though he were going to sit on the bench.

The kick was so swift he was certain the black giant would not see it, would only feel the smashing blow of Casca's boot into his testicles.

The blow was enough to bend any ordinary man over in agony, but it apparently did not faze the black giant who now came at Casca.

But Casca had not counted only on the kick. No sooner had the full force of his blow landed then his balled right fist was traveling toward the giant's neck, toward the voice box. The very momentum of the giant's own attack added to the blow, and Casca felt his arm almost jam back into its socket as it connected.

It was enough to momentarily stagger the giant, which was all Casca needed to smash the other fist full into the man's left eye.

The bottle of wine was lagniappe—pure luck that it should be available. The giant was still lunging forward, and Casca stooped down to avoid his rush—and caught the bottle with his free hand. Holding it by the neck, he jammed it into the giant's face. The glass broke, and splinters sliced across the flat nose and into the one good eye in a spray of wine and blood. Casca leaped aside, and the giant crashed into the bulkhead, going down. He went down completely when Casca smashed the back of his neck with a chopping blow of his right fist and followed that with as hard a kick into the man's kidneys as he could muster. The giant was now a silent heap at the foot of the door.

But Casca still had to get in the room. In the light of the ship's lantern he examined the door. Solid oak. He could see that it opened inward, which meant it was probably barred from within. A very heavy door, and it was fitted tightly all around with an edging of iron.

He made his decision and pulled one of the flasks out of his waistcoat pocket. He had not planned on using it here, but he had extra ones in the bearskin hat.

He dragged the unconscious giant out of the way, put the flask down at the bottom corner of the door, inserted the slow match fuse, and piled the two benches in front of it all. He lit the slow match with the ship's lantern, replaced the lantern and stepped back beyond the giant and lay down flat on the deck.

The gunpowder blew.

Casca was not an explosives expert. In the years since the invention of gunpowder he had had only some experience with the stuff, but that was it.

Yet whatever he did apparently worked. There was a terrific blast. Wood splinters flew everywhere. The ship's lantern was blown out. Smoke and fumes filled the companionway except for the narrow space down close to the deck where Casca was, and there was instant darkness.

But there was also a rough triangle of light where the door had been blown ajar, and it was toward this light that Casca propelled himself.

The door had only been blown off one hinge. The other, though twisted, still held. There was barely enough room for Casca to crawl in but he managed.

As he crawled into the cabin, he saw a girl tied to the stanchion. This must be Michelle, he thought. He also saw a nude female slave bound down on the table.

And he saw what Tarleton Duncan was getting ready to do to her—and knew what Tarleton Duncan really was, an animal of the worst kind.

There was no need for words. Casca pulled the short sword and lunged for Duncan, who dodged around the table, dropped the knife he had in his hand, and pulled a sword from a pair crossed on the bulkhead.

They went at it.

Casca cut, thrust, and parried Duncan's thrusts again and again. He worked with cold contempt, the way one would in killing vermin. He thrust.

Tarleton Duncan parried. They fought thus across the table, across the nude slave. The smoke from the gunpowder was now beginning to flow into the room—that and another smell.

Burning wood.

The blast had set the ship afire, as yet only in the companionway. But Casca, whose back was to the door he had blasted open, could now feel the intense heat. The door must be afire. He saw Tarleton Duncan's eyes flick toward the opening, and immediately the pirate captain began to edge his way around the table, fighting, but trying to retreat toward the heavily curtained stern window of the cabin.

Casca would not let him get away. Duncan was an excellent swordsman—but Casca's arm had had the experience of countless years, and the blade in his hand might just as well have been part of Casca's body. He not only fought Duncan to a standstill, he took the attack and pressed the pirate captain steadily back until he had him against the wall—against the side bulkhead, two steps away from the possible safety of the curtained window.

Duncan did not make any mistakes. In fact, he lunged suddenly, a perfect thrust that would have gone deep into Casca's guts had not the scar-faced one anticipated it and danced out of the way.

Then Duncan tried for the window.

He was too late. Casca's blade snapped the sword from his hands, and he was powerless. He stood motionless, a crafty look coming into his eyes as he anticipated the end of the fight, knowing full well that this one in front of him would not kill an unarmed man.

Casca, however, had seen what Duncan intended to do to the slave girl, and the question of whether or not to kill an unarmed man never occurred to him. The matter of destroying vermin did, however. He simply swung his sword quickly, the point slitting Duncan's throat from ear to ear. And, to make doubly sure, when the pirate captain started to fall forward, he made one quick thrust into the guts, turning and twisting the blade in order to sever the spinal cord and insure that this particular pirate captain would never get his jollies in his favorite way again. . . .

"Hell, Scarface," Katie whispered as she helped

Casca lower the unconscious Michelle—who had fainted at the shock of the battle—into the gig from the stern window, "you set the damn ship afire."

He turned back up to the stern window, to the frightened face of the naked slave he had cut loose from the table. Smoke was billowing all around her. "Get your ass down in the boat! Quick!" She climbed out the window and slid down the rope as ordered. Casca leaped for the second pair of oars. "Let's get the hell out of here."

It was none too soon. There was a sudden cry from on deck. Confused voices. They must have smelled the smoke.

"Row like hell, Scarface!" Katie suddenly said.

Stupid order. "Why?" he grunted.

"Because . . ." she said, straining at the oars, "I think I set . . . too short a . . . fuse!"

She had.

The gunpowder canisters she had placed and which she had lighted when she got the signal from Casca at the stern window—she had been lying in the gig waiting—suddenly blew. By then flames were licking up on the deck of the *Scorpion*. By the time they reached the sails they would also be at the powder magazine.

Casca and Katie rowed like hell. . . .

CHAPTER EIGHTEEN

Casca did not regret saving the young slave.

She had friends.

By morning he had the Portuguese ship under sail and standing out to sea—with an all black crew. Casca did not ask questions. He needed a crew and they fit the bill. That's all he cared about.

The young female slave was helpful, too. She took care of Michelle. A woman like Katie, Casca could handle—mostly because when you got right down to it Katie wasn't like a woman at all. More like a comrade.

Katie was the navigator. "Look, Scarface," she said, "we don't have charts for this part of the world, but I know this coast pretty well. Go north about fifty miles or so and there's this town—some damn name I can't say, but it begins with Saint Something-or-other, and likely as not we'll find a ship of some kind there that'll take you to Jamaica."

So they had started. But on the way, they had made friendly contact with a small sloop—a Brotherhood sloop—and Katie had known the captain. So Casca invited them aboard to have a friendly cup of wine.

And since the black crew had brought aboard new provisions, there was definitely a lot of wine to be drunk. The sloop captain was a young fellow, maybe twenty-five, and Casca liked him. For once Katie played the woman. After a couple of drinks she left the cabin to the men. Casca noticed this, but he didn't think much of it until after the sloop officers had left and the pirate ship had pulled away. He didn't see Katie. He went back to his own cabin, and the young female slave met him.

"Missy woman say give you this, Cap'n Long."

The letter was short, though the penmanship was bold and decisive:

> Scarface,
> It's been great fun, but it's just one of those things. I'm not ready for respectability. Yet. Give my regards to Jamaica, and maybe we'll cut across each other's bows some other time.
> Your obedient servant (Casca grinned at her writing "obedient servant")
>
> Katie Parnell

The blacks had helped him out of a spot, so when they got to the port Katie had indicated, Casca had the ship anchored offshore and he, Michelle, Big Jim, and Julio rowed to shore in the gig. What the blacks did with the ship from there on out was their affair.

A couple of days later he and Michelle were on a schooner—Casca thought it was one of McAdams' ships, though he could not be sure—as paying passengers on their way to Jamaica. He left Big Jim and Julio back at port. He would meet them after he finished his business with McAdams.

Michelle seemed to have recovered, but she was not the kind of woman Casca could get close to.

Or, maybe it was because Katie Parnell was still fresh in his mind. . . .

Any fears Casca might have had about the kind of man McAdams was were allayed when, almost at twilight, the stage stopped at McAdams' compound and the fatherly old Scotsman himself met them.

"Michelle! My poor Michelle!"

Casca watched the greeting. Admittedly he had been a little suspicious. An old man—and a rich old man at that—and a pretty young girl. I've seen too much of the dark side of life, he told himself. It will be good to move on.

And McAdams seemed equally appreciative of Casca—after he had welcomed Michelle, of course. At first he was surprised to see Cass Long. But the surprise quickly left his face. The man is obviously better than I thought. He insisted that Casca stay for dinner, but the scar-faced one was anxious to return to the coast, to go aboard ship and get some distance between them—though, of course, he did not tell McAdams that.

There was one thing, though, the pungent odor in the air, the smell of the boiling syrup in the sugar vats. Odd that it should be in the air this high up in the mountains.

McAdams caught the motion of Casca's nose, sniffing. He smiled. "A whim of a rich old man," he explained a little sheepishly. "I made my fortune in sugar, so I keep one small vat always boiling up here.

Irrational, I fear, but it's a relatively inexpensive peculiarity. The cost of transporting the cane up here from the fields is small. Besides, with all my money, why should I not spend it as I see fit?''

No argument there, Casca thought. Particularly since, in McAdams' office—next to the bedroom where Casca had entered weeks ago—before an ornate mahogany desk and in the light of a multi-candled chandelier, McAdams promptly paid him in gold exactly what he had promised.

''About Tarleton Duncan . . .''

''I assume you had to kill him.''

''Aye . . .''

''Unfortunate, of course. But when such a thing is necessary . . .'' McAdams let the words trail off.

Casca did end up staying for a mug of rum and for some discussion of the pirate situation. McAdams seemed genuinely glad that the concept of a Pirate Empire had run into snags, and Casca was ashamed that he had considered McAdams, like Governor Eden of North Carolina, might be involved with the pirates. Sitting in the office, watching the candlelight play on the lined face of the fatherly old Scotsman, he was reminded of the dim memory of his childhood and his own father—in Falerno, Italy, centuries before. . . . Bitterness welled in his heart, bitterness for not being like other men.

Abruptly he got to his feet.

''Ah!'' McAdams said. ''You must be anxious to be on your way . . . wherever it is.'' He called for a servant. It was now quite dark outside, the brief tropical twilight having given way to a dense, moonless night. "A toast for the road—and my thanks to you, Cass Long."

It was in the narrow stone corridor leading to the outside that Casca, a step behind the young slave who was his guide, first felt the dizziness.

Damn!

The "fatherly" McAdams had drugged that last mug of rum.

He stopped and stuck a finger as far down his throat as he could until he gagged, and then threw up. The slave who had been leading him looked back, fear in his black face. Casca retched as deeply as he could. But the drug had already begun to take effect. Everything before his eyes was blurring. He fought to keep from dropping into sleep. Damn! When the Jew gave his body power to repair wounds so he could stay alive, why hadn't there also been the power to resist drugs? Anger . . . Anger at the thought helped. He was still nearly blind, almost helpless, but the anger helped. He fought the weakness in his arms.

The salve who had been leading him suddenly took to his heels, running, shouting something that the dazed Casca could not quite make out. But Casca had enough sense to draw his sword. He leaned against the stone wall of the passageway, fighting the drug within him.

He could hear voices.

Arguing voices.

The drug effects were slowing. Some of his vision was coming back. Ahead of him, blurred but partially distinguishable, were the two who were supposed to waylay him—where the passageway was crossed by another. They had poked their heads around the corner. As Casca's vision cleared he could see the expressions of uncertainty in their faces. He waited. And they waited. The longer the minutes dragged by, the more the drug slowed in its power over his body.

But something was wrong—and he was too drugged to figure out what.

Then he knew.

Maybe it was the whisper of sound. Maybe it was the momentary flicker of expression in the eyes of one or the other of the two before him. Maybe it was simply knowledge gained from past experience. No matter. He heard.

And immediately dropped to one knee.

So the one slipping up so silently behind him in the passageway overshot his blow, the knife in his hand slicing close to Casca's head but missing it. His body tumbled over Casca's bent form.

Casca had no time for niceties. The drug still had a heavy effect on him—and there were three of them. He swung the sword quickly down at the side of his assailant's throat and was lucky. The head was neatly severed and began rolling like a ball down toward the two who were now rushing for Casca, swords drawn.

The rolling head of their compatriot gave both of them a little something to think about, so their attack on Casca was not quite as well-timed as it should have been. Casca rammed his own sword in the gut of one and immediately sidestepped, taking what cover there was behind the body of the dead man and letting go completely of his own sword. As he expected, the third assailant, presented with a moving target, slipped momentarily in the blood gushing from the stump of

the dead man's body, and the blow aimed at Casca
missed. Immediately Casca had him by the arm, pulling with all the failing strength in his still-drugged
body. Coupled with the slippery footing from the blood
it was enough. The man lost his balance and was falling
forward when Casca let go of him and chopped him
violently behind the ear with a balled fist. There was no
time to regain his own sword, so he picked up the
downed man's sword and brought the edge sharply
against the third man's face, slicing away the cheek
and cutting into the eye. But the man still wasn't dead.
Casca drove the sword into his kidneys, twisted the
blade, and pulled. After that he was sure the man had
lost interest in the proceedings. He kicked the other
dying man in the face, regained his sword, wiped it
clean on the man's clothing, and started to step around
the bodies.

That was when he heard the scream.

A woman's scream.

A scream of sheer terror.

There was no need for him to wonder who was doing
the screaming.

It could only be Michelle.

For a long moment Casca stood perfectly motionless
in the passageway. He had been wrong about
McAdams. He had delivered an innocent girl into a
madman's hands.

Hell!

But he had done his job. The girl was nothing to him.
It was none of his business. If McAdams wanted to
rape her, why, hell! let him rape away. Women had
been raped before. Dammit, he told himself, it's none
of my business.

But—

Oh, hell!

He turned and started back down the passageway, sheathing his sword.

CHAPTER NINETEEN

"Welcome back, Master Long!"

Casca spun on his heels and looked up at the balcony above him.

McAdams stood there hands on his hips, his expression that of one who has just heard an extremely amusing story.

"What's this all about, you son of a bitch? I did your job for you."

McAdams grinned benevolently. "Come up to my rooms and we'll discuss the matter."

Casca hesitated.

"What's the matter, Squire Long. You did come back to see me, didn't you? Well here I am. Come on up. No one will try to stop you."

Might as well get it over with. Won't find out what he has in mind until I do.

Men had gathered at the doorway but were held back by McAdams' command. "Let him alone. I'll call if I need you."

There was a tension to the house now that he hadn't noticed before. Perhaps it was caused by the sudden change in McAdams. When he'd told Casca to come on up, he was no longer the concerned relative who only wanted his lost relative back. There was now a heavy, pervading touch of evil to him that Casca had seen many times before. This was a sick man. Casca didn't know what his particular form of sickness was but he had the uneasy feeling that he would soon find out.

Cautious, he advanced up the steps past portraits of men who waited patiently on their canvases staring out at the world with eyes that never changed or faces that never grew old.

From McAdams' room Casca could hear a muffled sound issuing. He couldn't make it out clearly but he knew pain and fear when he heard it. There was something evil going on up there. His fingers tightened around the grip of his sword.

The door to McAdams' room was slightly open. A beam of light came from within. Casca hesitated a moment. Through the crack he could see McAdams sitting at his desk, waiting. *Come in said the spider to the fly.* "Well, man, are you going to stand out there all night?"

Casca gave the door a heavy kick with his foot just in case there was anyone standing behind it. The door bounced back. Only a quick movement of his left hand stopped it from shutting in his face. McAdams laughed pleasantly. "I don't blame you. I promise that none of my men will interrupt, at least not until I order them to."

The muffled sounds of pain were clearer now. Casca knew who it was making them without having to see. Michelle. But why?

He entered, closed the door behind him, and bolted it. He knew that there was no way he could keep out

McAdams' men for long but all too often a matter of seconds meant the difference between life and death. In the right-hand corner of the room on a low couch covered with a gold embroidered damask cloth, Michelle lay face down, her back bared where her gown had been ripped from her shoulders. Thin red streaks crisscrossed her back. His own welted hide twinged at the memory of his too-frequent beatings. The whipping had been done with either a thin reedlike cane or something similar. The skin wasn't broken but he knew the pain that the bastinado carried in its slender length. McAdams' mouth turned up a bit at the corner. He was obviously enjoying the whole scenario.

"You really are a sick son of a bitch, aren't you?" Casca growled as the awareness of just what McAdams really was began to come to him.

McAdams merely let the grin go all the way, his eyes lighting up with passion. "Sick? That is only a matter of opinion, my friend. To the contrary, I believe that the only sick thing in the world would be to deprive myself of the pleasures that I need."

Casca never took his eyes from McAdams. "Why?"

"Why did I try to have you stopped, or why did I bother having you return my niece to me?"

Casca had had just about enough bullshit. "Either tell me or get off your ass. I don't like to kill dogs that aren't on their feet."

"Don't be so impatient, Master Long. I told you my pleasures were important to me, and it pleased me at that minute to prevent your leaving. Depriving you of your wages and your life would have been quite a humorous moment for me. Just think, after all the trouble and danger you went through—to be killed at the moment of your reward.''

''Go on with it. What about Michelle? Why did you want me to bring her to you if this is all you had planned for her? Surely you have enough slaves that you could use for your pleasures?''

''Ahh, yes! There lies the rub. Simply put, the slaves belong to me because I have bought and paid for them. Michelle, however, is another matter. Since I first saw her in France when she was no more than a child I knew that I would have to have her one day. Therefore, in a manner of speaking, I paid for her too. Her father, my brother-in-law, never had two pence to rub together. I paid for her education, her clothes, her food—to have her molded into that which I desired. Everything she is I created. You should have seen her. A few months ago she was full of pride and arrogance, confident that no harm could ever touch her and not caring who else it came to. A fitting consort to a king.'' McAdams paused to catch his breath, his face growing red with the impassioned heat of telling his story.

''But that damned beast, Duncan, has cheated me! He has taken that which I reserved for myself. She has been spoiled. See how she cringes at my voice. She is good for nothing now save what few minuscule pieces of pleasure I may derive from her body and her pain.'' His voice rose to crescendo. ''I have been cheated do you hear?''

Casca knew now. McAdams was a madman who only fulfilled himself by the amount of suffering and horror he could inflict on others. Incest merely added to the spice of the terror he had planned for Michelle. He planned to abase her and break what remained of her mind and spirit. The whippings were just the first step in the training of his pet.

"What about Duncan?"

McAdams hissed. "Duncan had been my partner for many years and together we shared many pleasures among the captives he took. Most of his prizes came from information supplied by me and I would serve as the middleman for the disposal of the goods he captured. Through me he became rich and could have become the leader of the entire Brotherhood. But he betrayed me. He knew of my passion for my niece for we had talked many times over the years of how I had been so patiently awaiting her maturity—when she would be at exactly the right moment in her life for what I had planned. I should have seen the hunger in his eyes when I showed him her portraits as she grew into womanhood. When we had a parting of the ways, so to speak, he went after what he knew would distress me the most. He took the ship he carried her off in as a prize. I offered him much to have her brought back to me unspoiled. But he decided to keep her. Therefore I had to try and arrange a real rescue with you as my agent!"

McAdams closed his eyes, holding the lids tightly shut for a moment. He sighed almost sadly and said:

"That is the way of my life. Everyone I am good to always betrays me. But no more . . . Do not look so disgusted, Squire Long. You are a man who kills for money. There is little difference between us."

Casca started to move forward but was stopped by McAdams' upraised hand. "Hold it one moment, my friend. I have a thought. You have come back for revenge because I tried to have you robbed. Well if it's money you want, I can arrange for you to take Duncan's place. I will outfit you with the finest ship and guns that money can buy. Together we can take control of the Brotherhood of the Sea and rule the Caribbean as our own private lake, taking what we want when we want it. Now, how's that for a fine offer?''

McAdams knew that his offer had missed the mark when Casca started for him. His confidence that his wealth and the well-known greed of men gave him immunity passed rapidly as he saw the redness in Casca's eyes.

Scrambling back from his desk he came up with a rapier, slashing the air in front of him to keep Casca at bay. ''To me,'' he cried. ''Hurry!''

The response was immediate. Once Casca had shut and locked the door McAdams' hirelings had come to wait by it. Now they beat and pounded at the solid oak panels.

Casca was crawling over the desk, his sword beating back the more slender point of the lighter blade when the door gave. Four of McAdams' henchmen stumbled into the room, clubs and cutlasses in their hands. He had to turn away from McAdams to avoid a clumsy blow to his head with a club. When he did McAdams gave a cry of victory and lunged, running the slender blade all the way through Casca's back and out his chest. Casca jerked to avoid another strike by the same club. When he did McAdams' sword blade snapped near the ornate hilt. Casca didn't stop moving though the broken sword protruded from his front and back. He severed the wrist of the man with the club then caught him across his throat as he raised his sword back up to ward off the cutlass coming at his face.

Michelle was ignored during the fight. Crawling from her couch to a corner, she curled up into a fetal knot and awaited the outcome. She was sure it was going to be the death of the man who had saved her from Duncan only to deliver her to one even worse.

The remaining two men began to back away, fear of the crazy man before them on their faces and in their eyes. They couldn't understand why he kept coming at them slashing and cursing. He should have gone down by now.

One gathered enough courage to make a desperate lunge only to be kicked in the balls. The man doubled over in time to have his head half taken off. The other showed more sense and decided that McAdams didn't pay him enough money to die. He fled down the stairs into the dark not stopping till he was far away from the house where the devil with the sword through his body was on a rampage. Exhausted he sat under a tree to catch his breath, not aware of the eyes that watched him from the brush. The eyes were red-rimmed from the smoking of ganja. Maroons who had known his lash in the past would keep him company this night.

Meanwhile, McAdams rushed past shoving Casca to one side as he tried to escape. Casca caught his balance and followed. McAdams tried to find refuge. From across the nearest of his cane fields he saw a light coming from the warehouse where the sugar cane was boiled down. There were people there. He ran through the stubble of the fields which had only been cut down within the last week. He cursed his workers for it. He had no place to hide. Afraid to look back he could hear the dried cane stalks crushing under the steps of the one called Cass Long as the man gained on him.

At the edge of the field where the man-sized pots were boiling the work stopped as McAdams' hysterical form came out of the darkness. Around the vats were over a dozen black slaves, their dark hides oily with the effort of the night's warm work. Machetes or long cane knives hung at each man's side. To McAdams this was safety. Surely there was enough of them to stop the devil on his heels. Hurtling into their center between the large bubbling vats he cried out, "Stop him!" He pointed back to the stubbled fields where Casca was just entering the light cast by the cooking fires. "Stop him and you're all free men with gold in your pockets. I promise it. At the promise of freedom most of the men moved a few steps closer to the cane field, then stopped. Casca came at them, the broken sword still protruding from his chest, blood covering the front of his body as well as his hands and face.

McAdams screamed, "That's him! Kill him! Kill him and you and your families all go free." The blacks hesitated as Casca came at them, the weapons in their hands trembling. The dark beliefs of their native land were still too strong within them. Casca heard one of them whisper something hoarsely. It sounded a bit like, *Dumbala!* Then they all turned and fled leaving McAdams to face the demon alone.

McAdams couldn't run any further. His legs were more used to gripping the barrel of one of his fine chestnut geldings. Between two of the large vats he waited, legs barely able to hold his weight as fear and terror nearly paralyzed him. Casca came closer, his face reddened by the glow of the fires.

McAdams whimpered. He was used to being the one who inflicted terror and pain. This was wrong! "Why don't you die?" he sobbed. "Why don't you fall down!" Casca was only a step away. He dropped his sword and reached out his bloody hands for McAdams

and roughly pulled the man against his upper body
driving the point of McAdams' own broken sword into
the whimpering man's chest. Casca held him there like
a lover.

"I can't. . . ." Casca whispered in McAdams' ear
as he held him tightly in his arms.

McAdams screamed in agony as Casca pushed him
away off the point of the sword.

Then he shrieked again as strong scarred hands lifted
him off the ground till he was extended above Casca's
head. McAdams' mouth was already filling with blood
as he looked down to see that he was being raised over
one of the boiling sugar pots.

"Sweet Jesus! *No!*"

Casca dropped him into the thick bubbling substance. McAdams' screams were stopped when the
boiling sugar flowed into his open mouth. He tried to
stand and climb out of the vat but couldn't find the
strength, and the pain was impossible to imagine.
Raising his hands in front of his eyes he saw his own
skin peel away from the bone leaving clean skeletal
fingers. He slipped, this time silently, back into the
thick pungent mixture.

Casca pulled the rapier from his chest and tossed it in
the vat with what remained of McAdams. Not looking
back he recrossed the fields to the house.

By the time he'd returned to the house, the rest of
McAdams' guards had arrived. They didn't move.
Without McAdams to give them orders they didn't
know what to do. And a man doesn't risk his life for
pay when the paymaster is dead. They shrugged at
Casca and then exited out the front door.

Going back up the stairs Casca found Michelle still

trembling in the corner. Gently he took her hand and said softly, "It's all over." Half carrying her, he took her to her rooms and closed the door behind them. He laid her down on her bed where she instantly fell into the deep sleep of one whose soul needs rest. All the servants had left the house. Casca undressed her and found water and towels. Gently he cleansed her wounds then covered her with a sheet. He left the room for a time to do a little investigating through McAdams' personal papers, but when she awoke with the first light coming through the latticed windows, he was sitting at the edge of her bed.

"What happened?" she asked.

Casca stood. While she was sleeping he had taken the opportunity to clean himself as well, and was nowhere near the fearful apparition of the night before. "It's all over. McAdams is dead and you are now mistress here. He had no other relatives so you own all that was his."

Michelle rose up on one elbow. The sheet slipped away from her exposing one firm breast. She hadn't realized she was naked. But did she know that this strange man had not touched her during the night. There was an odd quality to him, a mixture of violence and gentleness that she hadn't seen in a man before.

Making no attempt to cover herself she reached out her own small hand and took the strong scarred paw of Casca. "I don't know what to do. Will you stay with me?"

Casca grinned to himself. She was a fine looking girl and she would need someone to help her. And after all he was in no great hurry. The Americas could wait a few days longer.

He would send word to Big Jim and Julio not to get impatient. He'd meet them soon enough.

"Yes, I'll stay for a time. . . ."

THE ETERNAL MERCENARY
By Barry Sadler

☐ 0-441-57295-2	**BLOOD RAID**	$2.75
☐ 0-441-57281-2	**BLOOD ULTIMATUM**	$2.50
☐ 0-441-57290-1	**CROSSFIRE RED**	$2.75
☐ 0-441-57282-0	**THE CYCLOPS CONSPIRACY**	$2.50
☐ 0-441-14222-2	**DEATH HAND PLAY**	$2.50
☐ 0-441-57292-8	**DEATH SQUAD**	$2.75
☐ 0-515-09055-7	**EAST OF HELL**	$2.75
☐ 0-441-21877-6	**THE EXECUTION EXCHANGE**	$2.50
☐ 0-441-57294-4	**HOLY WAR**	$2.75
☐ 0-441-45520-4	**THE KREMLIN KILL**	$2.50
☐ 0-441-24089-5	**LAST FLIGHT TO MOSCOW**	$2.50
☐ 0-441-51353-0	**THE MACAO MASSACRE**	$2.50
☐ 0-441-52276-9	**THE MAYAN CONNECTION**	$2.50
☐ 0-441-52510-5	**MERCENARY MOUNTAIN**	$2.50
☐ 0-441-57502-1	**NIGHT OF THE WARHEADS**	$2.50
☐ 0-441-58612-0	**THE NORMANDY CODE**	$2.50
☐ 0-441-57289-8	**OPERATION PETROGRAD**	$2.50
☐ 0-441-69180-3	**PURSUIT OF THE EAGLE**	$2.50
☐ 0-441-57287-1	**SLAUGHTER DAY**	$2.50
☐ 0-441-79831-4	**THE TARLOV CIPHER**	$2.50
☐ 0-441-57293-6	**THE TERROR CODE**	$2.75
☐ 0-441-57285-5	**TERROR TIMES TWO**	$2.50
☐ 0-441-57283-9	**TUNNEL FOR TRAITORS**	$2.50
☐ 0-515-09112-X	**KILLING GAMES**	$2.75
☐ 0-515-09214-2	**TERMS OF VENGEANCE**	$2.75
☐ 0-515-09168-5	**PRESSURE POINT**	$2.75
☐ 0-515-09255-X	**NIGHT OF THE CONDOR** (on sale November '87)	$2.75

Please send the titles I've checked above. Mail orders to:

BERKLEY PUBLISHING GROUP
390 Murray Hill Pkwy., Dept. B
East Rutherford, NJ 07073

NAME _____

ADDRESS _____

CITY _____

STATE _____ ZIP _____

Please allow 6 weeks for delivery.
Prices are subject to change without notice.

POSTAGE & HANDLING:
$1.00 for one book, $.25 for each
additional. Do not exceed $3.50.

BOOK TOTAL	$_____
SHIPPING & HANDLING	$_____
APPLICABLE SALES TAX (CA, NJ, NY, PA)	$_____
TOTAL AMOUNT DUE	$_____

PAYABLE IN US FUNDS.
(No cash orders accepted.)